SECOND BEST

Helen Cavanagh

SCHOLASTIC BOOK SERVICES
New York Toronto London Auckland Sydney Tokyo

A Wildfire Book

Cover Photo by Owen Brown

ISBN 0-590-32313-X

 Published by Scholastic Book Services, a division of Scholastic Inc.

12 11 10 9 8 7 6 5 4 3 2 1 9 1 2 3 4 5 6/8

Printed in the U.S.A. 01

Chapter 1

Shelly Barr curled her fingers inward, hiding them, as she watched her older sister lightly tap long, well-shaped fingernails on the blue-print tablecloth. Linda's nails symbolized her to a T, Shelly thought bitterly: polished and perfect. Quickly she looked down, struggling with the ugly thought that followed: *I hate her!*

Immediately a denial welled up inside her. *No! I love her! She's beautiful, the best sister in the world.* Still, she kept her eyes lowered until gradually the sound of her mother's cheerful, husky voice and her father's answering laughter brought her back fully and she was able to look up and smile.

Usually, just after dinner was Shelly's favorite time, especially when it was cold and blustery outside as it was this March night. The large homey dining room with Tony's old upright piano at the far end had seemed for all of her sixteen years like the very heart of the big old house on the hill. It was the room where the family came together at mealtimes and on special occasions to celebrate the day and each other. Sometimes, after dinner, with everyone sitting together, the hanging Tiffany lamp casting a rosy glow over the seven people at the heavy round table, Shelly felt such a strong sense of love and utter contentment that it brought tears to her eyes.

Now, sipping her coffee, light and sweet the way she liked it, Shelly felt some of that good feeling return and she relaxed slightly, thinking about her family: for instance, how each member was expressed in the choice of an after-dinner beverage.

Shelly thought: Mom and I like our coffee with lots of milk and maybe too much sugar because neither of us really likes the taste of coffee that much, but we do like to be sociable and now it's such a comfortable habit. When she was little, her father used to pour a smidgin of coffee into her milk and she remembered how it made her feel very grown up.

She didn't understand how her father could like his coffee black, although, of course, she knew his reasons. He liked his drinks either piping hot or icy cold and anything in-between annoyed him. Plus he was on a diet again. Her father's frequent diets deprived him of bread and potatoes but somehow allowed him a large slice of pie before he went to bed.

And Tony. He used a little milk but he firmly disapproved of sugar. Her brother, now seventeen, had subscribed to *Good Health* magazine for three years now. Sugar, he often said, was the cause of most of our modern-day ills.

And there was Linda with her clear, sugarless tea with only a wedge of fresh lemon for flavor. It set her apart from the rest of the family but it did suit her, Shelly thought, her eyes scanning her sister's lovely face framed by long, fair, naturally curly hair. Even now, after a full day of classes at Chancellor School of Design and the wearing commute to and from Boston, Linda looked fresh and elegant, her silky cream shirt spotless. Shelly was suddenly uncomfortably aware of the grimy cuffs on her own blue cotton shirt.

The twins still drank milk. Eric, six minutes younger and seven pounds lighter than Angela, dabbled his small fingers in his beloved yellow ducky cup, singing softly to himself while his more determined twin drank her milk in one long, noisy swallow.

"More milk, Sheddy," Angela demanded, banging her pink cup.

Shelly made a face at her but got up quickly, laughing. What a devil her baby sister was. A little devil with an angelic name.

The twins were almost like her own babies. When they were born two years ago, her mother had welcomed her help eagerly. Sometimes Shelly thought her mother shouldn't have had another child at age forty, and certainly not two. Although Louise Barr was still young looking and attractive, Shelly knew how tired and frazzled she was after a day of twin chasing. But now, looking at the babies, so sweet with their fine blonde hair and rosy skin, Shelly was awfully glad they had been born.

She poured more milk for Angela and was rewarded by a tender pat on the arm.

"My good girl," Angela crooned.

Eric's milk was on its way to the floor so Shelly removed it quickly, replacing it with the wooden butter-dish cover which he pounced on delightedly. Shelly sat down again and caught Linda's eyes appraising her.

"What?" she asked.

There was a hint of exasperation in Linda's voice. "You have a button missing."

Then in a kinder tone: "If you can find it, I'll sew it on for you later."

Shelly nodded. It was always like that with Linda. One minute she felt put down, angry; the next she was grateful for her sister's helpfulness. Long ago, she had decided that Linda didn't try to be mean. It was just that sometimes — in fact, most times — she was thoughtless. Besides that, she was superconscious of any kind of sloppiness. Even her mother came in for some of Linda's criticism, but her mother always just laughed it off and kept on doing things the way she always did them, casually and cheerfully.

But it isn't so easy for me to laugh it off anymore, Shelly thought. Not when you're sixteen and trying to be the best person you can be. Not when it really matters what people think of you. She wished that things like hairstyling and makeup and grooming were second nature with her as they seemed to be with Linda. For Shelly, who had to cope with fine, straight, light-brown hair and sensitive skin, it just didn't seem fair that her sister should have been born with so much. Somehow, even her mother's pep talks which pointed up Shelly's enormous hazel eyes and her "adorable" nose failed to comfort her.

And that business about her feet.

Linda was tall, as tall as Shelly, but their bones were different. Linda was like her father: small-boned, small-featured, well-proportioned. Shelly took after her mother: broad-shouldered, slim-hipped, almost boyish in build.

Anyway, it was the feet incident that Shelly was thinking about now and a flash of fresh hurt coursed through her and she didn't dare look up from her coffee.

Linda and Shelly were shoe shopping at Sterns. Linda tried on several pairs of shoes and every one looked great on her and finally she ended up buying two pair. Then it was Shelly's turn. She had wanted a certain pair of brown leather shoes with wood platforms for a long, long time and Stearns had them in stock. She pointed them out to the salesman.

"Size 10, please."

When he brought them to her and she slipped them on, she looked up and glanced at Linda. Her sister's shoulders were shaking and her face was convulsed with suppressed laughter.

"What's the matter?"

"I'm sorry," Linda managed, almost choking. "I can't help it. I mean, *those* shoes — in size 10!"

She laughed openly, helplessly.

"Shelly, do you think we'll be able to carry them on the bus?"

She whooped with laughter, causing several other customers to look over and smile along with her.

Shelly looked down at her feet. The shoes *were* big. Monstrous. The wood and leather, instead of looking smart and stylish, suddenly looked grotesque, and her feet in them, long and freakish. She wavered between embarrassment and deep hurt but then pride took over and she managed a laugh.

"I know," she said. "You can carry one and I'll carry the other."

She went ahead and bought the shoes but whenever she wore them now she felt big and awkward and ugly. Before that, she had accepted her big feet the same way she had accepted the rest of her body. Now, ever since that day, Shelly was aware of all her imperfections. It didn't help that her father had comforted her about her feet.

"Don't worry, honey," he had said. "You'll always have good balance."

It was the same kind of reassurance she had received from her mother when she complained about being so small on top.

"Don't think about it so much. It's not important. Anyway, remember, you'll always look *neat.*"

Deep down, in that quiet place where she had always kept her secret thoughts and feelings, Shelly knew how much she minded not being like Linda. Linda had everything: looks, brains, talent, and good habits. Next to her, if someone were to compare them, Shelly knew she would always come out second best, and it hurt.

It did help at moments like this to think of Ryan.

Ryan Gallagher thought she was pretty and nice to be with. He told his friends that Shelly was his "Number One Girl," so that must mean he was proud of her. And he said he liked her long brown hair.

"Don't cut it, ever. It's so shiny and pretty," he had said.

She treasured that compliment because Ryan didn't say things like that very often. Even after almost a year of being around her, he was still kind of shy about saying sweet things.

For that reason, she had made a list of his rare, special words and when she read down the list, it sounded to her almost like poetry. She knew the whole page by heart.

"You're so real, Shelly. You're nice to be with."

"Keep on smiling, girl; it makes me feel good."

"You know? Everyone likes you."

"I like your quiet moods too. When I'm tired, it's nice."

"You always make me laugh at everything."

Last on the list were the words she treasured most:

"I love you."

He had said that one night after everyone else had gone to bed. He was getting ready to leave and he was complaining about having to go out in the cold after the cozy warmth of the fire. Suddenly he reached out and folded her in his long arms. He held her close to him for just a moment, long enough for her to put her head on his shoulder and then he lifted her face and kissed her softly. When he pulled away, his face was serious.

"I love you," he whispered.

She remembered the feeling of tenderness for him at that moment and how she had touched his cheek before she answered.

"I love you, too."

Since that time, he had called her or come over almost every day. That wasn't always so easy with the hours he worked at the garage. Often he was so tired that he was ready for bed as soon as he got home. Still, he always made time for her and now he always ended his visits or phone calls with those words.

"I love you, Shelly."

"Is Ryan coming over tonight?"

Her brother's question coming on top of her private thoughts made Shelly jump and her father smile.

"Shelly's off in her own world again. Give her a chance to come back to us, Tony."

Her father chuckled and stood up.

"If anyone wants me, I'll be in my study. Good dinner, Lou."

Tony was looking at her, waiting.

"He said he was. Probably any minute now."

"Good. I want to show him something."

"Oh, so now you're going to hog him all night."

"Nah. I have to study for a psych test. Anyway, he's my friend too. I knew him first. You're the one who hogs him."

Her mother laughed. "I'll have to tell Ryan about this conversation. He ought to be flattered that you two are fighting over him."

For a minute, Shelly thought of the two books on the telephone table: *Blue Whales* and *Giants In Peril.* She had taken them out of the school library today with such good intentions. She had chosen whales for her English research paper.

Miss Abbott was surprised but when Shelly explained how interested she was in the plight of the huge mammals who were being slaughtered by the thousands each year and how several groups were fighting to save them from extinction, her teacher had urged her to find out more. Just thinking about the project excited her. She had planned another trip to the Boston Public Library over the weekend for more books on the subject.

But if Ryan was coming over —

If she helped her mother with the dishes —

If she got the twins ready for bed as she loved to do —

Then she wouldn't have much time for reading. Maybe she could tell Ryan about it, let him know that she really should —

The doorbell rang and instantly Angela clapped her hands.

"Hello, hello," she yelled happily.

"It's Ryan," Shelly said and quickly set Eric down on the floor and hurried to get Angela down too. Immediately the toddlers started for the door and Shelly couldn't help laughing at the way they vied with each other for first place.

All at once Eric stopped, his eyes on Linda, his face lighting up. He stood beside her and reached out a tiny hand. Shelly saw what he was looking at: the three delicate gold chains around Linda's neck. Eric loved jewelry.

Linda bent her head toward the little boy and Shelly paused to see what her sister would do. She felt a start of surprise when Linda reached down and picked Eric up, setting him in her lap.

"You like my chains? See, Eric — pretty."

Shelly's heart softened. Her sister really was all right. She could have bet just a minute before that Linda wouldn't let Eric on her, especially before he was cleaned up. Although she knew her sister loved the twins, she also was aware that Linda had little patience for their natural messiness.

She left the room smiling to herself. Yes, Linda was all right.

Ryan stood on the front porch, his dark blonde hair freshly brushed. Shelly knew immediately he had just washed it. A few times he had come over straight from work and he had looked so cute then, grease smeared on him from head to toe. But tonight he was *gorgeous*, Shelly thought, and smiled at him.

"I thought you were never going to let me in," he said grinning. "Don't you know it's cold out here?"

"Come in then," Shelly said, taking his big rough hand and pulling him into the front hall. "You're letting the outside in."

For a minute she debated about giving him a hello kiss but her father's study opened off the hall and the door was partway open. She felt kind of shy about kissing in front of her parents. Not that they would mind, she thought. They were always kissing and hugging around the house. But some things were private, she decided. Besides, she knew Ryan. With his quickness to blush, he'd probably get embarrassed. Instead she squeezed his hand and pulled him toward the kitchen.

Then she heard it.

The sudden shriek and then the thin wail of terror.

Eric!

She dropped Ryan's hand and ran toward the sound. There was Linda, white-faced, standing beside her chair. Eric stood too, his eyes wide and frightened, sobbing as if his heart would break.

Her mother ran in from the kitchen and stopped in the doorway, her eyes anxious.

Shelly ran to Eric and scooped him up. "Take it easy, honey," she said. "It's all right."

To her sister she whispered: "What happened?"

"Look at me," Linda wailed. "My new skirt."

Shelly looked. A wide dark stain covered the

front of the beige flannel skirt. She knew immediately what had happened. Eric was still new to his training pants and he had wet on his sister — an unpardonable sin.

"Boo-boo," Eric cried, holding up his little arm to her.

Then Shelly saw the marks. Four crescent-shaped indentations, shockingly red on the delicate skin. Linda, in her shock, must have dug her nails into Eric's arm, she thought.

"Look," Shelly said, holding out his arm for her sister to see. "Look what you did to him."

She was torn with pity for the frightened baby in her arms.

"Oh, I'm sorry, Eric." Linda's face was very white. "I didn't mean to do that. It was just that — it was so unexpected." She held the offending skirt away from her body.

Linda's mouth trembled and for once she seemed to lose her poise.

"I'm sorry, Eric," she said again and hurried from the room.

Her mother came and took her son from Shelly's arms. He stopped crying and began to play with his mother's gold hoop earrings.

The moment of panic was over. Shelly knew the marks would disappear, probably by morning. Before she turned to Ryan who stood in the doorway, Shelly thought again of her sister's nails, reminding her of her earlier observation. Polished and perfect, she had called them. But she knew now that they could hurt too.

For this moment anyway, she didn't think she wanted to be *exactly* like her sister.

Chapter 2

While Tony and Ryan talked cars and engines in the cellar, Shelly led the twins up the dark wooden staircase, stopping as they always did on the first landing at the big double window.

"Where's the moon tonight, kids?" she asked.

Angela pressed her nose against the glass and gazed straight ahead, her mouth turning up at the corners impishly.

"No moon," she said. "Moon all gone."

"Silly — look *up*," Shelly said patiently. They played this same game often.

Eric was sleepy and he leaned against her, his thumb in his mouth.

"Make a wish, Eric," she said.

Her father laughed at Shelly's insistence that you should wish on the moon, not a star. Her mother said it wasn't so strange.

"The moon has been a symbol of womanhood since ancient times; you're probably right in preferring it," she had said.

"I wish Mister Monkey go sleep," Eric said, removing his thumb for a moment.

"Mister Monkey's waiting for you, Eric. When you go to sleep, he'll go to sleep too and then you'll get your wish," Shelly promised him.

Eric sucked his thumb harder, nodding his head contentedly.

Angela tugged at Shelly's sleeve.

"I wish I stay up and play," she said firmly.

Shelly laughed. "Good try, Angie," she said, leading them the rest of the way up the stairs.

She ran warm water in the big claw-footed bathtub and undressed the twins quickly, chatting all the while. She lifted them one at a time into the water and started Eric first.

Angela started to wash her own face and then suddenly she flopped over on her stomach and laid her face directly in the water. Before Shelly could say anything, Angela had her whole head underwater and bubbles appeared on the surface. She sat up again and blinking, she grinned delightedly at Shelly.

Angela has absolutely no fear, Shelly thought. She'll try anything.

I was like that too, she remembered suddenly. I always climbed to the top branch of a tree and leaped across chasms and fast-rushing streams. Tony and I always did stuff like that when we were little. Mom and Dad never minded except sometimes when we tore up our clothes or lost our sneakers.

She wondered if Eric would always be so timid and shy and sensitive and if Angela would be as full of vim and daring as she was now at two.

It's funny, she thought as she soaped Eric's legs and feet, of all of us, Linda is the only one who never really liked to play. In her memory, Linda always preferred to stay in the house or yard with her books and drawing stuff or later with her beloved paper dolls. She couldn't for the life of her remember Linda with torn pants or dirty socks.

She finished with Eric and checked Angela. The little girl handed Shelly the washcloth and pointed to her back. She had washed everything else. Shelly washed her small back quickly. She took them out of the tub and wrapped them in towels. One by one, she dried them thoroughly, taking time to do "This little piggy . . ." for both of them. She reached for the folded night diapers in the old-fashioned bureau next to the sink. Angela took one look and backed away, another familiar game.

"Eric baby," she said pouting, "Angie not."

Angela never had an accident during the day as Eric sometimes did, but just as she played hard, she slept very deeply and without nighttime protection her bed was often wet in the morning. It never fazed her. She always just said, "Eric did it."

Shelly picked her up firmly and laid her down on the thick bath mat.

"Come on, Numkin — let Shelly fix you. Just tonight."

Reluctantly, Angela accepted her fate but grabbed the baby powder from Shelly's hand.

"Angie do it," she said and sprinkled powder liberally on her own body, Shelly's, and before she could stop her, on the floor around her.

Shelly made a mad face at her and Angela giggled.

"Look what your sister did to me, Eric," Shelly said, shaking her head and brushing the white stuff from her jeans. Eric smiled at her sweetly.

She led them to their bedroom and found warm, footed pajamas and dressed them quickly. Eric was even sleepier after the warm bath and she had to lift him into his little bed. His eyelids were heavy — just about closed — but one small arm reached out for his stuffed monkey who was waiting, as Shelly promised, on his pillow.

Mister Monkey was held and stroked tenderly, but in a matter of seconds Eric was sound asleep. Shelly gazed down at her little brother and smiled. What a little angel, she thought.

Angela had her head in the toy box, both arms out of sight when Shelly scooped her up.

"Okay, babe — to bed. No fooling around now. Ryan's downstairs."

"Angie stay up too." She tried again, her head tilted hopefully.

"No, Angela. It's really sleeping time."

With that, the tiny girl climbed onto her bed and punched the pillow as hard as she could. She wriggled down under the covers and lay stiff and straight on her back. She squinched her eyes up tight.

"Me sleepin', Sheddy," she said in a loud whisper.

"Good girl," Shelly said, kissing her cheek. "You're a good girl and Shelly loves you."

She tiptoed from the room, turned off the light, and left the door open halfway. She stood in the hall for a long moment, enjoying the clean baby smell that was strong in the warm air. She felt herself smiling. Being with the twins always made her feel good. Partly because they needed her, she thought, and partly because — well — babies are just beautiful. She realized suddenly that her mother had said that same thing to her once.

But I feel that way too, she thought now. I love the look of complete trust in their eyes and the way they learn so quickly and get excited about simple little things. I love the look of them, the feel, even the smell of them. It must be true. Like Mom often says, I'm a born mother.

Were all women, she wondered? Was it really an instinct or something? She wasn't sure. She had seen mothers in the market yanking their children around roughly, threatening them, calling them awful names. Was that mother-love? And there were plenty of women who had no children and seemed perfectly content. She thought of fathers, too. She had seen some who were cool and distant, never home and not upset because they weren't, but she knew some fathers, including her own, who were warm and tender with their children, even, sometimes, more than the mothers. If there is an instinct, then men can have it too, she decided. Loving babies and kids doesn't depend on whether you're a man or a woman. It just depends on what kind of person you are. Satisfied, she walked down the long stairway, humming to herself softly.

Ryan was sitting at the kitchen table with Tony, a large mince pie between them. Louise Barr stood at the sink, her pretty face flushed with heat and laughter.

"The guys just made a deal with me," she said. "If they can have another piece of pie, they'll finish the dishes. What do you think, Shelly?"

"Definitely," Shelly answered. "They just made you an offer you can't refuse. Ryan should wash though. It softens his hands."

She smiled slyly at Tony. "Tony has to dry, except I'm going to watch him. He thinks one quick swipe with the towel and the dishes are done. It takes him less than three minutes."

Tony cut a generous slice of pie for Ryan and then one for himself.

"Look who's talking. It takes you *two* minutes and the silverware never gets put away."

Mrs. Barr dried her hands on the towel and reached for the hand lotion.

"I shouldn't really let you do dishes, Ryan. You worked today, didn't you?"

"Yes, I did. Only I don't mind. I do them at home when Mom's fighting to meet a deadline. Besides, like Shelly said, the hot soapy water does them good."

Ryan's rough, sore hands worried Shelly. She knew working on cars meant grease and oil and the soap they supplied at the garage worked pretty well to get the worst of it off, except the hand scrubbing, especially during the winter months, caused severe chapping. Whenever he came over, Shelly poured hand lotion generously on his hands, sometimes rubbing it in for him. The first time she did that, Ryan had teased her.

"I know," he said, "just an excuse to hold my hands."

It was true in a way. She like his strong hands in hers but her main concern was even simpler than that. She just wanted him to feel better.

"How is your mother, Ryan?" Mrs. Barr asked. "I don't see her very often but I do read her articles every week in *The Towncrier*."

"She's fine," Ryan said. "Busy. She's either at

the typewriter or at a town meeting. She's always complaining that the paper pays her peanuts and every week she says she's going to quit, but she won't. She loves what she's doing."

Kitty Gallagher, as her byline read, was the local reporter for the small weekly newspaper which was delivered house to house every Wednesday. Shelly had heard Dad say that Kitty was a good writer. "Better than some of the big-name journalists," he had commented often, but Ryan explained that his mother didn't have the confidence yet to try a city paper.

"Up until the time Dad died she had only done poetry and a few short stories. She sold a couple of confessions when I was little, but that was all. After the funeral, though, she figured out the money situation and it was pretty bad. She saw an ad for a reporter and she tried for it. The editor was a nice guy and he gave her a chance. The first article she did took her about five hours and it was only about two pages long. Now she knocks off an eight-page story in forty-five minutes."

Shelly had recognized the pride in Ryan's voice when he spoke of his mother, although she had also heard him complain about her lackadaisical housekeeping.

"Anyway," he had told her, "she figures she's losing money now because she's fast. She gets paid by the hour, you see."

Ryan didn't make much of the fact, but Shelly knew he contributed most of his weekly pay to the household, saving only enough money to buy gas and oil for his ten-year-old car and occasional hamburger and movie money for his dates with her.

Knowing this made her content to stay home and have him come over most of the time. It didn't matter where they were, or whether he was spending money on her. She was proud of him for helping his mother keep a home together. She liked him even more when she saw the way he treated his twelve-year-old sister, Kathleen.

She remembered how carefully he had shopped for her at Christmastime, making sure she had at least three or four packages from him to open. He would never admit it but the reason he had to wash his jeans every night of the week was because he was down to one good pair. Shelly had seen Kathleen recently in a pretty, red hooded jacket and she had known immediately that Ryan had bought it for her.

Shelly was happy too that her parents approved of Ryan. They were both friendly and easy with him, treating him like one of the family. Even before Shelly and Ryan started going together, when Ryan was just Tony's good friend, her father had called him "levelheaded" and "a mechanical genius." Her mother agreed right from the start that he was good-looking and nice to be around. Tony, of course, thought he was wonderful, and the twins loved him. Only Linda, with one of her double-edged remarks, said: "He's certainly nice enough, Shelly — but don't you mind? His fingernails are always so black."

Leave it to Linda to judge a person by something like that, Shelly thought now, remembering her own inner anger at the time. She hadn't answered her sister then, but she still held that remark against Linda.

At that moment her sister entered the kitchen, looking almost impossibly beautiful in her long blue-green velour bathrobe. Her long hair showed the marks of a very recent brushing and the blonde waves were perfect. She smiled, showing small, even teeth, and asked pleasantly: "Can I help, Mom?"

Mrs. Barr looked at Linda appreciatively. Shelly had seen that look often in her mother's and other people's eyes when they looked at Linda. She really was lovely.

"When the fellas get straightened out here, you can put the dishes away," Mrs. Barr said. "Would you like some pie before these vultures devour it completely?"

Linda shook her head. "No thanks. Just some milk, I guess."

Shelly watched her sister go to the refrigerator and take out the container of skim milk she shared with her father. Linda didn't have any weight problem but she told Shelly it was good for the complexion.

She poured milk in a glass gracefully and Shelly envied her for her easy poise. No one would ever guess that only an hour before Linda had been all shook up.

Looking away from Linda, Shelly glanced briefly at Ryan, and then, as she was about to look away, she stopped and stared at him hard, her heart suddenly sinking in her chest.

Ryan had his chin in his hand, his pie forgotten and his gaze directed at Linda, his eyes dreamy. He didn't even notice Shelly's hard stare.

She felt a sickness spread through her stomach.

It felt like poison rushing through her system, affecting every part of her body, even her arms and hands. There was a huge lump in her throat and she swallowed hard. All at once she knew what this horrid feeling was — she had had it before. Jealousy. But not like this! Never as strong or as powerful as this!

She felt terrible. Ryan. Her own loyal, wonderful Ryan looking at Linda like that. It wasn't fair! Linda had everything. She couldn't have Ryan too!

Any minute now she would cry. She could feel the tears coming. She swallowed again, fighting for control.

Just then Ryan seemed to come to with a start and he looked down at his pie, picked up his fork and resumed eating. When he looked up he noticed Shelly looking at him and he winked at her.

The green poison began to recede slowly and the awful sick feeling it brought left her. When she looked at her hands, she was amazed to see them so tightly clenched. She relaxed them slowly, carefully.

Linda moved to the old-fashioned pantry off the kitchen where the ironing board was kept. Shelly knew she would be busy pressing tomorrow's outfit for awhile and would be within earshot. But she promised herself that as soon as she and Ryan were alone, she would ask him about that look he had given Linda. Maybe she shouldn't. Maybe it was stupid to show him that it bothered her so much. And maybe, too, she wouldn't like his answer. But she had to know: Was Ryan in love with her sister?

Chapter 3

"No!" Ryan said emphatically. "What's the matter with you?"

Shelly tried to control her trembling bottom lip.

"I just thought — I mean, I saw you looking at her like — "

She stopped, unable to continue. Ryan looked surprised but — did she imagine it? — just a little sheepish.

"Just because I looked at Linda — and I guess maybe I did — doesn't mean I *love* her, Shelly." He lowered his voice. "I'm not even sure I *like* her."

They were alone in the big kitchen. Her mother had just made fresh coffee and cut a piece of pie for her father, and now she knew her parents were sitting together on the couch in front of the fire, enjoying what was left of the evening, and each other. On some nights Shelly joined them, but essentially it was their private time and she left them alone.

When Ryan came over, she usually entertained him in the large, cozy kitchen where they could snack and talk and laugh without disturbing anyone. Now they weren't laughing.

"What do you mean?" she asked him. "What don't you like about her?"

"I guess what I mean is — Linda scares me."

Shelly snorted.

"She does, really. A guy can't help but look because, well, she is pretty. But then, after you look awhile, you get the feeling that she's not really human."

He shrugged impatiently. "I'm not explaining it right. Shelly, you know how you look at pictures in a magazine? A picture catches your eye and you look at it for awhile. But then you turn the page and forget it. It doesn't really have anything to do with your life. Linda's like that — like someone in a magazine. I never know what to say to her."

Shelly was surprised. Ryan didn't analyze feelings like that.

"Maybe it's because she's older?" Shelly suggested.

"Nah. Only a year, anyway. It's what I said before. She's not *real.* She's like a model or even a movie star. She has nothing to do with me."

He must have seen the look on her face.

"Don't be sad, Shelly. You're my type." He grinned and tickled her under the chin. "Are you going to fish for more compliments now?"

"No," Shelly answered, inwardly satisfied, "but it would be nice to look like something out of a magazine and not out of a comic book."

She made a horrible face and stuck out her tongue.

Ryan laughed. "That's why I love you, Shelly. You *are* so real."

When Ryan left — kissing her twice by the front hall closet — Shelly decided to sit with her parents for just a few minutes. She watched the tail end of the news on TV and the weather report and then she stood up and stretched.

"Good night, Mom, good night, Dad," she said, kissing each of them in turn.

"Hey, how's school these days, Shel? I haven't talked to you in so long," her father asked. His face was downcast but there was a crinkling around his bright-blue eyes that meant he was teasing.

Did fathers get jealous when their daughters found boyfriends? Certainly it took away from the time they spent together, she thought. Before Ryan, she remembered, she and her father held long, satisfying conversations in his study, amidst a clutter of blueprints and stacks of papers covered with numbers. Thornton Barr, a civil engineer, thought nothing of bringing his work home with him; he always had. Plus now he was doing some consulting work on the side to bring in extra money.

Enfield, a suburb of Boston, was an expensive place to live, Shelly knew. The homes were large and lovely and the downtown section was attractive and well-kept. Their own three-story, brown, shingled house on the hill had been a good buy fifteen years ago from what her father had said, but her mother had confided once in a rare outburst of despair: "This house is a white elephant now. Who would ever want to buy it?"

Shelly had known without asking that her mother

was referring to the sagging, cracked ceilings on the first floor and the old-fashioned plumbing, not to mention the kitchen that was in the process of being "remodeled" and had been for at least five years. Her father was tops in his field, highly intelligent in all matters that concerned him, but home improvement never seemed to get finished.

When a room needed paint or a faucet leaked, her mother and now Tony usually tended to it. Shelly knew how to use a hammer and screwdriver too.

If her father was a casual handyman, then her mother had to be his equal in the housekeeping department. The upstairs hall was a mishmash of odd bureaus, lamps, books, laundry baskets, and assorted boxes of things her mother couldn't bear to throw away. Like her mother before her, Louise Barr was a saver.

When her grandmother died three years ago, her mother made many trips to her Boston apartment and spent many hours sorting and packing her mother's belongings, intending to give away or sell most of it. In the end, she couldn't bring herself to do it. Shelly smiled, remembering. At least one bedroom and a good portion of the upstairs sunporch and the hall had been given over to her grandmother's "things," with her mother promising every other day to "deal with it."

Shelly had seen her mother spend whole afternoons going through the boxes, only to pack everything back without discarding a thing.

"It all will be important someday," she explained. "A whole life's history is there."

Her mother had loved her mother deeply and

now she spoke of her longingly, recalling for Shelly and Linda, and whoever would listen, episodes of her grandmother's long life. Although her grandmother had a Boston address, she spent weekends and holidays at the Barrs' and now, Shelly thought, it still didn't seem right without her.

Shelly climbed the narrow flight of stairs that led to the third floor where she and Linda each had their own bedroom and shared a bathroom. Linda's door was closed as usual, a sign that she was asleep or she wanted privacy.

It's funny, Shelly thought, I hardly ever close my door. Maybe that's because I'm basically nosy and I'm afraid of missing something. She smiled to herself. No, she thought. It's because I like to feel part of everything. The sounds of family life going on below, the twins calling to her sometimes, the phone ringing, the faint drone of the television set were all music that made her feel safe and warm.

"Shelly?"

It was Linda, opening her door, her voice low.

"Shelly, if you're thinking of taking your bath now, you'll have to take the clothes rack out of the tub. Don't forget to put it back; my sweater is still drippy."

Her voice sounded so honestly concerned that Shelly almost laughed. Linda's handwashing — her underwear, sweaters, and best blouses — always seemed to fill the bathroom. She never let her dirty clothes pile up the way Shelly did. Right now, Shelly would bet that every single piece of clothing Linda owned — except for the sweater now drying — was clean and folded neatly in her drawer or hung in perfect alignment in her closet.

Shelly nodded agreeably. There was no reason to argue or make fun as she was often tempted to do. Besides, she had already decided not to take a bath tonight; a quick wash-up would do. Only she wasn't going to admit that to Linda. She would be horrified.

Linda smiled slightly. "Want to see something?" she asked. "I just finished it."

She stepped back and Shelly entered her sister's private domain. The room was different from the rest of the big house; there was an almost exotic strangeness about it. Maybe it had something to do with its perfect neatness.

The bed was the focal point. Linda had dressed it in a cool lavender — sheets, comforter, and dust ruffle. She had covered a half dozen throw pillows in crisp, creamy eyelet. It looks so nice and inviting, Shelly thought, thinking of her own big bed with its rumpled sheets and old patchwork quilt.

Linda led the way to the far end of the L-shaped room which was furnished with a sewing machine, cutting table, desk, and drawing board. Her father had managed to get the board at a good price from his company and had presented it to Linda on her fourteenth birthday. It was her most treasured possession, Shelly knew. She remembered Linda saying: "It's so wonderful to know that Mom and Dad take me seriously as a designer."

There was no question that her sister was talented — that had been obvious even when she was a little girl. But it wasn't just her artistic ability. Linda had an endless supply of fashion ideas, a sense of rightness about fabrics and trims, and perfect good taste. Add to that her attention to detail and constant work and yes, Linda was already a fashion designer.

Shelly looked at Linda questioningly.

"What did you want to show me?"

Suddenly Linda looked hesitant, almost shy.

"My project. I have to pass it in tomorrow. Designs for a bridal party. I chose to do something nontraditional. I hope Mr. Frank will like it."

With that she removed a blank sheet from the top of a stack of paper and began arranging her drawings for Shelly to see.

The wedding dress caught and held Shelly's eye first and she gazed at it with honest appreciation. It was beautiful but Linda was right, Shelly thought. It was not your usual bride's dress.

It was outstanding for it's simplicity. It had a high, Mandarin collar and long, fitted sleeves, and the long skirt was molded closely to the body. The veil, however, was big and billowy, surrounding the figure like a cloud. Although it was just a drawing, the dress material had been drawn with extreme care and it gave the impression of thin delicacy.

"Silk. A very fine silk," Linda said, as if reading Shelly's thoughts. "Here, I'll show you."

She went to her closet and withdrew a pale, silk blouse, classically styled, the kind she always made and wore. Shelly fingered it carefully, admiring not only the fineness of the material but the scent that rose from it. Her sister's closet, bureau drawers, and even Linda herself smelled that way. It was a rather odd odor, pungent and distinctive, but appealing. Shelly knew its name: Patchouli, an essence oil that now almost everyone associated with Linda. Once Mrs. Smirnak, the librarian, told Shelly that she knew whenever Linda Barr was in the library. "I don't have to see her; her perfume always gives her away," she had said.

Shelly looked now at the other costumes: maid of honor, bridesmaids, flower girl. The colors Linda had chosen were unusual for a wedding — a pure, sunny yellow, a hot pink, a bright emerald green. Still for all their brightness they didn't overshadow the bridal dress. Shelly told Linda that.

"Good. I'm so glad you said that. That's the thing I was a little worried about. The bride should always be the central figure."

Shelly made another observation. "All these," she said, her hand sweeping the drawings, "are they supposed to have sort of an East Indian flavor? That's the impression I get."

"Oh, exactly. Great, Shelly. I'm glad I showed you. You said just the right things."

Linda was beaming at her and Shelly returned her smile, but suddenly, inside, she felt tired and depressed. On top of that, she felt a small rush of that green sensation and she was ashamed. She *was* proud of Linda; she *did* admire her work. Couldn't she give her sister a simple, deserved compliment without these awful jealous feelings? A mean little voice always seemed to be whispering inside her head, *Why can't it be me?*

"I know Mr. Frank will love these, Linda. I really do," she said as sincerely as she could.

She kept smiling until she felt the smile getting ragged at the edges and then she moved toward the door.

"I'm beat, Lin — I'd better get ready for bed now. See ya."

Once in her own room, she turned and shut the door firmly. Tonight — right now — she wanted to be alone. She needed time to sort out all the disturbing feelings she had had today.

Life is really good, she began. I'm really so lucky! It was something she often said to herself lately, the words like a talisman against problems. And I don't really have any problems, she continued. Not like other kids at school. Kids she knew who really had something to worry about like divorced or alcoholic parents or like Dorrie Redoff with her mother in a mental hospital. As she undressed she counted up all the good things in her life: her mother, her father, Ryan, Tony, the twins, this nice old house, her friends, school, good health. I'm really lucky, she repeated, then stopped suddenly in the middle of putting on her pajama top. I forgot Linda, she thought guiltily. I listed everything and everyone and I forgot Linda.

She sat down heavily on the edge of her rumpled bed. I guess that tells me I really do have a problem, she thought grimly. My problem is that I'm a mean, jealous, rotten person! I don't deserve what I have!

Shelly crept under the quilt and snaked her hand over and turned out the light. No washing her face tonight, Shelly decided. Almost as if she believed her thoughts could transform her features, she did not want to see her face in the bathroom mirror. Somehow, she knew that tonight she would look as ugly as she felt inside.

Chapter 4

It was very dark with the door closed. The March wind blowing through the top branches of the big trees caused them to brush against the side of the house. The sound comforted Shelly.

Her grandmother had called the third-floor room her "haven" and had written a poem about it which had been framed and hung now above the heavy maple bed. Her grandmother had really loved this small room; how had she put it?

"The room I chose was not a grand affair,
But small and simple, and beneath the eaves;
Though I had stairs to climb, I did not care,
For I could hear the rustle of the leaves — "

When her grandmother first wrote that poem she had read it to Shelly, but later Shelly read it many times herself, so that now she knew it by heart.

For a long time — as long as she could remember — whenever her grandmother came to visit Shelly slept with her in this bed. When she died, the little room became totally hers, but even now, three years later, she thought of it as "Grandma's Haven."

Lying in the darkness now, still feeling miserable about herself, Shelly felt a surge of longing. If only Grandma were still here I could talk it over with her, she thought. Afterward, she'd hug me the way she always did and say exactly the right thing. Her mother was good, she listened well, she was always interested; but sometimes she seemed to lecture. Her grandmother had never done that, or at least not so you noticed. What she did was tell you a story, usually from her own life, that illustrated her point, and then she would manage to make you see the silliness of a situation. Before you knew it you would be laughing hard and wondering what you had been so upset about in the first place.

Grandma, in appearance, had been the very image of what a storybook grandmother should look like, Shelly thought, huddling deeper into her quilt. Small and slightly plump with wavy gray hair and glasses. Cuddly-looking and warm. But when you really knew her, Shelly thought, you realized that while she may have looked like the typical little old lady, she was no such thing.

Sometimes Shelly had thought that she, Shelly, was the only one who knew what the *real* Katherine Taylor Marchant was like. Did anyone — even Mom — know she hoarded Juicy Fruit gum in her stocking drawer and when she was alone chawed on three or four pieces at a time? Or that words were her biggest passion and she considered the completion of a difficult crossword puzzle or the writing of a poem two of the most exciting things in her life? Or that she dearly loved to arm wrestle or feet-fight in bed? Shelly had a clear picture of her grandmother, breathless and giggling, clad in freshly ironed pink pajamas, demonstrating the crazy, complicated dances of her youth.

She wondered now if her mother even knew that a year after her grandfather died — long before Shelly was born — a darkly handsome Irishman had proposed to her grandmother.

One night, after a long bedtime conversation with the light out, her grandmother had told her about Sean Corcoran.

"I could have loved him easily," she told Shelly. "He was such a sweetheart of a man." She had sighed. "But I thought he drank too much and I thought he was sure to ruin himself and anyone near him. I had your mother and your uncle Johnny to worry about."

Shelly remembered the long quiet space between that part of the story and her grandmother's laughing voice that followed.

"Come to think of it, maybe a little ruining would have done me good back then. I was such a righteous little prig."

"What's a prig?" Shelly had wanted to know.

"You know, a whatchamacallit, a goody-goody. Yes, looking back on it, I should have married Sean."

Shelly had tried to comfort her.

"Good judgment, Grandma. You always tell me how important good judgment is."

"That's right, honeybunch. Only mine wasn't very good. Sean Corcoran married a classmate of mine from Wellesley and went on to become a United States Senator. They have four lovely sons." Her voice had been wistful in the dark.

"But Grandma," Shelly offered, "you had Grandfather at least. You told me he was wonderful."

Her grandmother had turned on her side and put both arms around her and held her tight.

"Bless you, Shelly. You always say exactly the right thing."

Remembering brought a lump to Shelly's throat but also a feeling of deep pleasure. Mom was right, Shelly thought. Talking, or even just thinking, about someone who has died is good. For a few moments Shelly had managed to bring her grandmother back and she didn't feel quite so alone anymore.

Still, now, she tossed and turned in the big bed, unable to find a comfortable spot. Maybe it was because she didn't feel so comfortable inside. It would be so nice if she could just go to sleep and forget.

Forget that at least three times in one evening she had hated her own sister. Who could she admit that to? Only her grandmother would have understood. Her mother would listen carefully and she would try to understand, but Shelly knew it would upset her inside. Her mother disliked any kind of unpleasantness. Knowing that had stopped Shelly many times from being completely honest or openly angry. It was perhaps the only thing that she resented about her mother. It would be better, she thought, healthier, if you could get good and mad, even screaming mad, but that kind of temperament was simply not tolerated in the Barr household.

Many times she had wanted to scream and shout, even kick some pots and pans about. Hey, there was a poem, she thought ruefully, and then punched her pillow as hard as she could.

Immediately, Angela's little face popped into her mind. Why, her baby sister had done exactly the same thing tonight. And for the same reason: frustration.

Shelly rolled over on her side, bent her knees almost up to her chest, and for the first time since she got into bed felt herself begin to relax.

Pillow-punching isn't bad at all, she thought sleepily. If only —

Her mother's urgent voice woke her abruptly, but she held on tightly to the remaining threads of a beautiful dream. In the dream she had just been presented with the Nobel Prize for — what? She burrowed her head under the pillow, desperately seeking the answer.

"Shelly. Get up this minute. You're going to be late for school," her mother called up the stairs.

Shelly gave up and opened her eyes slowly. Usually her mother didn't have to call her; the alarm was the first morning sound she heard. The alarm. Oh, no, she had forgotten to set it last night! She looked now at the clock and sat upright in bed, panicked.

Only twenty minutes to wash, dress, eat, and catch the school bus. Wow, it was going to be a close one this morning, she thought.

She hurried to the bathroom, gave her face a fast scrub and rinse, brushed her teeth, and looked around frantically for her hairbrush. Not here. Then she remembered it was in her purse on the hall table downstairs. No time for it. She dashed into Linda's room and saw her brush and comb arranged just so on her bureau. Too rushed to feel guilty, she used it, mentally noting as she did that her hair needed washing. Tonight, she promised herself. She pulled the telltale brown hairs from the brush and replaced it.

She ran back to her own room and yanked the closet door open. Her heart sank. Except for a couple of dressy things, the hangers were empty. In a panic, she tried to remember the last time she had ironed. She pictured the pantry and the baskets loaded with clean clothes. No time to press anything now, though.

The full hamper in the corner of her closet caught her eye. It was more than full; it was jam-packed. That meant all her sweaters and jerseys and shirts were dirty. Hoping against hope, she left the closet and rummaged through her bureau drawers. She found last year's bathing suit, the white sweater she had shrunk to doll-size, and some torn underwear good only for the ragbag. Great! Now what was she going to wear?

The jeans she had worn yesterday were tossed carelessly over the desk chair and she inspected them quickly. Not too bad, but what on top? She glanced at the clock. Twelve minutes gone. *What was she going to do?*

The picture of Linda's well-ordered, well-stocked closet just across the hall flashed into her mind. Too bad Linda's already gone — I could borrow something. Since she wasn't home, Shelly couldn't just take —

She knew Linda would have a fit. Linda didn't lend clothes easily and Shelly had never just helped herself. But she *had* to now. It was an emergency!

She stood just inside Linda's closet, conscious of that distinctive perfume, and flipped quickly through almost two feet of blouses and tops. She noted they were arranged precisely according to color.

Her eye caught sight of a pale beige long-sleeved shirt. She thought of her own good camel slacks and made up her mind. It wouldn't hurt to dress up a little for school today.

She grabbed the blouse and ran back into her room and in two minutes she was dressed. She hesitated in her doorway, feeling unfinished somehow, and then remembered her lipstick. That was in her purse downstairs too. Oh well, she decided quickly, I'll fix up on the bus.

She bounded down the two flights of stairs, grabbed her jacket from the closet, her purse and gloves from the hall table, yelled "so long" to her mother and the twins, and ran out the door and on down the hill. The cold air shocked her at first but she forced herself to run fast, ignoring the mad thudding of her heart. She had only three minutes to get to the bus stop. She ran hard, and even in the cold air, she could feel the perspiration forming under her arms.

Oh, no. Linda's blouse!

On top of that thought came another one, even more horrible.

I forgot deodorant!

Guilt and panic set in at once and she opened her jacket wide, hoping the fresh air would stop her from sweating. She caught a glimpse of the yellow bus stopped at the end of the street and she increased her speed. Her friend Sandy was waving her arms and Shelly could see her mouth form the word *Hurry*.

She reached the corner just as the last person had boarded. She bolted up the bus stairs, panting, her breath gone.

Sandy laughed at her openly. "You were a sight, Shel. Why don't you go out for track?"

She managed a grin but she couldn't stop thinking about the blouse. Had she smelled it up? Linda would absolutely kill her and Mom would be mad at her too. What a way to start a day, Shelly thought. She had the awful feeling that it wasn't going to get any better either.

But her mood began to improve as the morning went on. Once in school, with classes to go to and friends to talk with in the halls, she almost forgot about the blouse except for an occasional twinge of guilt. Finally, after a few such bad moments, Shelly decided that while Linda would definitely be angry at first, when she explained her early morning predicament, her sister would soften and forgive her.

By the time she reached English class just before lunch, Shelly was able to laugh and talk normally with the other kids until Miss Abbott called the class to order.

Miss Abbott was her favorite teacher: young, pretty, with lustrous dark hair and large dark eyes that made Shelly think of the big black olives Dad liked so much.

But it wasn't only her looks that impressed her or made Shelly and every other student like junior English so much. It was her way of teaching that somehow made learning something to look forward to every day.

Janet Abbott shared her own likes and dislikes,

her philosophy, parts of her personal life, past and present, and her zest for life and anything beautiful with her students. She had a knack for weaving all aspects of life with the subject she taught, saying, "Everything is connected." Her special enthusiasm for anything to do with books or language was catching.

Even boys who had always considered English dull liked her class and their marks improved. As Leo Hughes, Enfield High's star wrestler, put it: "The woman makes sense. I understand what she's saying." No one laughed either when Leo, who looked like a bull with his heavy shoulders and thick chest, wrote what Miss Abbott declared "a very sensitive poem."

Almost magically, Janet Abbott had the power to bring out the best in everyone she came in contact with. Maybe it was just because you always got the feeling she cared about you as an individual, Shelly thought, watching her now.

"I hope you all have been enjoying the reading and research for your projects," she said. "To me, that's the best part of this kind of assignment. It comes bit by bit, almost like you're doing a jigsaw puzzle. The pieces start to fall into place. Suddenly, you are able to see the subject as a whole."

She grinned suddenly.

"At least, I *hope* you are all at that point because I certainly have given you enough time. By now you should be well into the writing. You all know the deadline — a week from tomorrow," she said.

Miss Abbott talked with her hands, a trait that she said she inherited from her British father and *not* from her Italian mother.

Shelly had listened to her teacher's pep talk with a growing feeling of dismay. She thought of the two books on the hall table that she hadn't yet opened. All she had done so far was read a couple of magazine articles about whales and a short chapter from an old book she found in her father's study.

For this project, Miss Abbott had given strict rules, including how to write a bibliography that included at least six sources. She also wanted footnotes.

Suddenly Shelly felt almost sick with shame and despair. What's the matter with me, anyway? she questioned herself silently. I fiddle and faddle around, getting absolutely nothing done. I make great plans to do something — to really accomplish something — and what happens? Nothing! I'm just impossible, that's all. If she could have, she would have put her head down on her desk and bawled. Miss Abbott had given them plenty of time.

She couldn't stop yelling at herself mentally. Disorganized, lazy, sloppy, dumb — What had she said last night? That she was lucky? That she didn't have any problems compared to some other kids? Baloney! At least the other kids did their work when they were supposed to. I flub up on everything, she thought hopelessly.

"— but if you haven't quite done all your reading yet, don't panic and give up. You can still do it and write and meet the deadline," Miss Abbott was saying.

"People aren't all alike. Not everyone works at the same speed or in the same way. Some of us procrastinate all over the place or take more time to absorb knowledge," she said good-naturedly.

"What I really mean to say is, don't worry. Just do your best and make this research project worthwhile for your own sake."

Miss Abbott ended her speech and turned her attention to Kim Decker, who had her hand up.

Shelly's spirits had risen during her teacher's remarks and the hopeless feeling had somehow changed to a renewed hope.

I'll do it, she promised herself, almost saying it out loud. I'm not dumb really. I'm just one of those people she talked about — a procrastinator. I go at things differently, that's all.

A cherished compliment her father had once given her popped into her mind and it fed her spirits even more.

Once, after a long conversation with her father, covering many subjects, he had leaned back in his swivel chair and declared positively, "Shelly, you have a darn good brain!"

She remembered now the glow of pleasure it had given her and her own reply: "I must take after you, then."

Now the thought of *Blue Whales* and *Giants In Peril* waiting for her at home seemed to offer a challenge. Reading them no longer seemed like an impossible task. She would begin right away, the minute she got home from school. After supper she would go straight to what was now *her* haven and read until at least one book was finished. She would do the same thing tomorrow and then on Saturday she would take the trolley into Boston and spend the day at the public library. By Monday, she planned, she would be writing. Far from being behind with her work, she felt fine now, almost ahead of herself.

By the time the bell rang signaling the end of class, Shelly felt really good. She smiled warmly at Miss Abbott on her way out, wishing that she could hug her instead. She couldn't wait now for school to be over so she could get started. This was going to be the best work she had ever done in her life.

She fell into step with Sandy and Kim and walked toward the cafeteria, nodding and smiling happily at the kids she knew in the noisy, milling crowd. She loved feeling so strong and capable. Everything was great. She had been such a jerk to worry so much about everything.

Chapter 5

Shelly took one look at Sandy struggling with the plastic ketchup dispenser and burst out laughing.

"You think it's so funny?" Sandy asked, making a disgusted face. "Why do they have these darn things here anyway? They're impossible."

She kept squeezing the dispenser with no results. "By the time I get anything out of here, my hamburger will be ice cold."

"Patience, my child, patience," Shelly said piously, trying to hide her laughter.

"Here, let me do it," Donna Englehardt said matter-of-factly. "There's a trick to it."

Sandy handed the dispenser across the table gratefully.

"My mother hates those things," Shelly offered. "She won't have them in the house."

Donna fooled with the cover, banged it hard against the table, pressed the sides a few times, and then pointed the nozzle toward Sandy's hamburger and squeezed.

Whooosh! Ketchup erupted from the plastic bottle without warning, spraying the table and it's occupants with the blood-red mixture. Screams of horror immediately changed to squeals of hysterical laughter.

"You look so funny — it's in your eyebrows!"

"Yeah? Well, it's all over your face."

Shelly laughed hardest at the guilty look on Donna's face.

"I thought I put the cover on tight," she said.

Shelly and Sandy giggled helplessly as Kim ran her tongue over her chin and finding ketchup there, murmured, "Mmmm-good."

Shelly was still enjoying the spectacle when Mrs. Osgood, the elderly cafeteria aide, came over to the table.

"Here's a wet rag, girls. Better mop that mess up quick."

She squinted her eyes in Shelly's direction. "You better get some cold water on your blouse right away," she said. "Ketchup stains, you know."

Shelly dropped her eyes quickly and gasped. "Oh, no!" she cried.

The entire front of the beige shirt was dotted with blobs of the red stuff — small spots, but spots just the same.

Mrs. Osgood clucked with her tongue. "Better get a move on, dear. Else it will be ruined."

She grabbed her purse and books and stood up, pushing her chair back so abruptly that it clattered to the floor.

The girls looked at her questioningly, their faces serious now.

"It's not my blouse — *it's Linda's,*" Shelly explained, close to tears.

Immediately, Sandy stood up. "Come on, Shel. I'll come with you. If we get 'em fast, it'll be okay."

Shelly was grateful to her friend and let herself be led to the girls' room. She had never really discussed her feelings about Linda with Sandy, even though she considered her her best friend, yet Sandy seemed now to understand the seriousness of the situation.

Ketchup, mustard, even a whole pot of spaghetti sauce on one of my own blouses would be really funny, Shelly thought. Now, a few spots of red on the pale blouse spelled catastrophe. Her good mood, the feeling of hopefulness, was gone, replaced by a terrible uneasiness.

Mrs. Osgood and Sandy had better be right. If cold water would solve the problem, she wouldn't care if she had to walk around the rest of the school day soaking wet. If not — if the stains wouldn't come out —

Sandy looked at her, one eyebrow raised. "You're really upset, aren't you, Shel? You look like you're going to cry. Take it easy, will you? It's not *that* bad."

"You don't know my sister," Shelly said grimly.

"I don't know — maybe I do," Sandy said quietly, adding, "But she's certainly not going to kill you, so stop looking like you're going to your death."

"Okay," Shelly said, managing a smile, "but let's get it clean. *Then* I'll feel better."

Between the two of them, a generous application of icy water, and a handful of the harsh school soap, the spots came out — almost.

Looking closely, Shelly could still see faint orange smudges where the spots had been. They decided finally that they would completely disappear with a proper washing at home.

"The minute I get home I'll do it, dry it, iron it,

and put it back in her closet. I won't even have to tell her," she told Sandy.

The sense of foreboding faded as she hurried to study hall. The only thing is, she thought, I'll never do that again. I learned my lesson.

By the time school was over and she joined Sandy for the bus ride home, she had some of her good spirits back. After all, as her friend had said, no one was going to kill her!

The twins looked bewildered as she raced past them up the stairs, taking time only for a breathless "Hi, kids." Usually her homecoming was a joyous time for the babies. Her mother had told her how they positioned themselves at the big window on the stairs and waited patiently for her to come over the hill. Shelly had always allowed time for kisses and piggyback rides, ending with a juice and cookie snack at the kitchen table.

But today she went directly to her bathroom, stripped off the shirt and threw it over the edge of the tub. She ran warm water in the sink, adding a generous dollop of liquid detergent. She heard the phone ring twice downstairs and then, within a minute, her mother's voice calling her.

"Shelly, come quickly."

She turned off the water and ran down the third floor stairs and leaned over the banister.

Louise Barr's voice shook. "That was the school nurse. Tony got hurt in machine shop and they've taken him to the emergency room. She said it didn't seem too serious but that he would probably require stitches. I've got to go to the hospital right now, Shelly. I've got to see for myself."

Shelly tried to reassure her mother but she knew from experience that comforting words weren't enough. Her mother was like a tiger about her children. She could be fierce in her protectiveness and nothing could keep her away if one of them was hurt.

"Go ahead then, Mom. I'll put some clothes on and be right down."

"Thanks, dear," Mrs. Barr said, heading for the coat closet. She stopped. "Oh, and Shelly, I have a roast ready for the oven. Put it in at four. Oh, and I promised Tony I'd make the potatoes his favorite way. Would you peel some and par-boil them for ten minutes before you add them to the roast? And Eric's pants need changing, I'm afraid."

She looked up at Shelly. "I'm sorry, honey, to put so much on you the minute you walk in the door. I don't know what I'd do without you."

Shelly smiled down at her mother. "Don't worry about it. I'll take care of everything. You go and see how Tony is. Just give me a minute to throw on something."

She grabbed a gray sweater from the top of her hamper and pulled it over her head. She could hear Eric crying so she hurried.

"I'm coming, Eric," she yelled as she took the stairs two at a time. "Shelly's right here with you."

Angela and Eric were playing contentedly with blocks in a corner of the kitchen and Shelly was just putting the roast in the oven when she heard the front door open and close. Mom and Tony must be home. Good. If they were that quick, it probably wasn't anything too serious —

"Hi. How's everything?"

Linda's voice drifted in from the hall and Shelly heard her heels on the stairs. *She was going right up to her room.*

Shelly froze, the heavy roast still in her hands, the oven door open. The shirt — evidence of her crime — still lay on the edge of the tub. If Linda performed according to habit, the bathroom was the first place she would stop to wash the grime of the day from her lovely hands.

The heat from the preset oven poured out at her but it couldn't touch the growing coldness in the pit of her stomach or soothe the sudden tenseness in her neck and shoulders. She slid the pan onto the rack and shut the oven door. She straightened and stood silently, waiting. Any minute now she would hear —

"Motherrrr!"

Linda's voice coming from high up was shrill and piercing enough to cause both babies to look up, startled.

And then Linda was hurrying down the stairs, her heels clattering. She burst into the kitchen, the offending shirt in her hands. She looked around for her mother, her angry eyes finally focusing in on Shelly.

"Are you responsible for this? Did you do this?" Her voice was shaking with indignation. She didn't give Shelly a chance to answer.

"Of all the nervy, sneaky things to do. It's not enough that you take it without asking, but to bring it back dirty and *smelly* — " Her voice rose to a high-pitched shriek.

Linda stared down at the shirt in her hands. She

raised her eyes to Shelly. They held a look of total disbelief. "Why, there's — *there's even a ring around the collar!*"

The tenseness left suddenly. The worst had happened. Linda had discovered her deed, was very angry, and probably would be for quite awhile. But it wasn't the end of the world. Everyone would survive — even Linda. She *was* sorry. Taking the darn shirt had caused all kinds of trouble and worry. It was a big mistake, she thought. Something she wouldn't repeat. She tried to tell Linda this, tried to apologize, but her sister didn't seem to be even listening.

At the same time, in a corner of her mind, Shelly marveled at the intensity of Linda's concern for a single piece of clothing, and in still another part of her mind was a very real sense of shame mingled with resentment caused by Linda's comments about her personal habits. While it was true she had skipped a bath last night she knew she certainly wasn't that dirty, nor did she *smell* even without a deodorant. She shouldn't let anyone degrade her like that — no matter what she had done!

She cut in above Linda's sudden threat to "discuss this subject with Mom and Dad."

"Go right ahead, Linda. I said I was sorry — what more can I do?" Shelly eyed her sister coldly, aware of her own growing feeling of anger.

Linda glared at her. "Okay, I'll tell you what. You keep this." She tossed the shirt toward Shelly. "I don't want it anymore. I hope you enjoy it."

She whirled around and left the room at high speed.

Shelly felt like she could explode with anger but

glancing at the silent, staring twins, she made an effort to be calm. Managing what she hoped was a cheerful grin, she scooped up the shirt from the floor. Okay! If that's the way Linda wanted it, she would keep it, wear it, and enjoy it. Kim and Donna had said she looked nice today, and it wouldn't bother her at all if there were little orange dots on it forever.

In fact, Linda could go fry ice for all she cared. At least, she decided, her own concerns were more important and worthwhile. She reassured the twins by telling them a silly story and soon she had them laughing.

By the time her mother and Tony came home, everything was fine. Tony's self-conscious grin was an indication that while he liked the attention, he felt a little foolish, not only about the accident but because the wound had only required two stitches.

"Big deal," he said before he disappeared into the cellar to commune with his beloved engines and tools.

Shelly had decided she wouldn't tell her mother about the scene with her sister unless Linda did. Her mother had had enough worry for one day. But, she decided at the same time, she would not walk around looking guilty all night either.

There is such a thing as pride, she thought, and dignity. Linda walks all over mine and doesn't think twice about it. Shelly's sense of personal dignity helped her through dinner — a meal that seemed endless, with her sister sitting stony-faced across the table.

Shelly's efforts to be casual and gay with her family left her exhausted, though, and depressed.

When Ryan came, Shelly was relieved when Tony captured most of his attention with enthusiastic plans for modifying one of his newer engines.

Once Ryan leaned over and whispered, "Everything okay?" She nodded "yes," but she was glad when he said he had to leave early to study for a test.

"Tomorrow's Friday, Shelly. How about a movie after supper?" he asked just before he left.

Wearily, Shelly thought of her plans for reading the rest of the week. But right now the thought of concentrating on anything beyond a hot bath was too much.

"Sure, Ryan. That would be great," she answered, trying to sound normal.

When he left, kissing her sweetly, she climbed the stairs slowly, listlessly, not even comforted by Ryan's obvious concern for her.

Maybe tomorrow night she could talk to him, tell him what was going on and how it made her feel. Maybe just talking about it would make it all easier. Maybe, like her grandmother used to do, Ryan could help her to see the funny side of it, make her laugh and wonder why she let Linda upset her so much. Only right now she didn't feel much like laughing.

It wouldn't help to cry either, she decided. Besides, she was much too tired. As she shut the door to her bedroom, she wondered how it was possible to feel so old when she was only sixteen. In fact, she didn't think even really old people ever felt quite this ancient.

Chapter 6

Never mind, she thought — today I'm really getting down to business. She would let nothing interfere with her reading this afternoon.

Cuddled up under the warm quilt, two big pillows behind her, a dish of raisins at her hand, *Blue Whales* opened at page 94, she felt secure and happy, knowing that she was finally spending her time well.

She should not have allowed herself to get so depressed yesterday, nor should she have worried about today. What was it that Grandma used to repeat so often? She remembered now:

"Today is the tomorrow you worried about yesterday and all is well."

It was true, she thought. It was stupid to let things bother you so much. Worrying just made things worse. It was better to think positively and trust everything would turn out for the best.

She directed her attention to page 95 and almost immediately was caught up again with the whales and the ocean. It was exciting, she thought, and sad too. Helping to save these wonderful creatures would be so worthwhile. For a moment she let herself imagine a whole summer on a ship. She would become a member of Greenpeace — the organization who sought to save the whales from hunters and extinction. She was touched by a description of members caressing a dying whale, trying to ease his agony, not letting him die alone. These people really cared, she thought now, cared about all living things probably. That's what I want, she decided, looking up for a moment. I want to help someone. Someday I'm going to do something really worthwhile.

The book was so interesting that she lost all track of time and she was honestly surprised when she heard her mother calling her for supper. Sure enough, her clock read six. Only a few pages remained of the chapter and she lingered under the quilt still reading until she heard her father's voice boom up the stairs.

"Shelly! Now!"

She knew her father wouldn't start eating until the family was all seated and he hated lukewarm food, so she hurried.

There was excitement in the air and Shelly sensed it immediately. She looked at her mother questioningly.

"What's up? she asked.

Her father and mother looked very pleased about something. Her mother's face was flushed, her eyes were bright, and she couldn't seem to stop smiling.

"Hurry up and sit down, Shel," Tony said. "Mom said she has an announcement to make."

Shelly's mouth dropped.

"Oh, Mom. Are you — ?" She didn't finish the question, just let it hang there.

Louise Barr looked confused for a minute and then threw back her head and laughed merrily.

"Did you hear that, Thorn?" she asked, gasping the words out amid peals of laughter.

"Shelly thinks I'm pregnant again. Poor darling, she looks like she's going to faint."

"No, Shelly," Mr. Barr answered, smiling at her. "The twins are quite enough right now. The announcement we have to make concerns Linda."

Linda's eyes suddenly became very wide and alert and she leaned forward eagerly.

"Mom, Dad — tell me. What is it?"

Mrs. Barr took an envelope from under her plate. It was long and creamy white and as she held it up, Shelly could see in bold black letters the return address: The Chancellor School of Design.

"It's a letter for us about you. It's from Dean Stoessler," her mother said.

"You said it was good news, didn't you, Mom?" Linda asked.

"I *didn't* say," Mrs. Barr said with a twinkle in her eye. "But you don't think we'd be so happy and silly if it was bad news, do you?"

"Motherrr," Linda said urgently. "*Read it.*" Her pretty face was tense.

"All right. Here goes." She unfolded the letter and then suddenly handed it to her husband.

"I'm much too excited. You read it," she said.

Mr. Barr cleared his throat and began — very slowly.

"My dear Mr. and Mrs. Barr — " He paused.

"Dad," Linda moaned.

"Okay, sweetie," he said and began to read normally but Shelly noticed he pronounced each word carefully for maximum effect.

"I am pleased to tell you that your daughter, Linda, will receive the coveted Polli Darnell Scholarship enabling her to spend this coming summer in New York City studying under Ms. Darnell herself."

A wave of excited "oh's" swept the room.

Her father continued: "When a student shows exceptional promise we send samples of her work to outstanding designers in the hope that just such work/study programs will be offered.

"The period of study will begin on June 20th and will continue through August 15th and will be cost free. Linda's room, board, and a reasonable allowance will be provided for under a term of the scholarship. Arrangements may be made for suitable accommodations, perhaps at a reputable hotel catering to young career women."

The letter continued for another few lines but no one was listening.

"Polli Darnell," Linda breathed, her eyes wide. "I can't believe it. Mom, do you know who she is?" she said.

Her mother snorted. "Do I know? I know that Bonwit's carries her dresses and I know what they cost! She *has* to be the best!"

Her father beamed at Linda. "Someday it's going to be your dresses in all the best stores. I can see it all now — Linda Leigh Barr — Designer Extraordinaire — Toast of New York, Paris, Rome — "

Shelly looked at her parents, their handsome faces alive with pride and dreams. She looked at her sister, who sat still, her face changing from moment to moment. One second it was glowing, radiant, and the next a cloud of doubt descended.

"Polli Darnell," she said. "I've read she's really *formidable*. Very fussy. One article said she once fired a seamstress for using the wrong machine stitch."

Shelly saw the naked fear in Linda's face and hurried to reassure her.

"Don't worry, Linda. You're so careful about your work you won't have a bit of trouble. I know you won't."

"Gee, New York City," Tony broke in. "What a break. My sister living in the Big Apple. All those famous places and people," he said dreamily.

"And you'll be famous too, Linda," Shelly declared positively, determined to be nice and make this moment as happy as possible. That's what families are for, she thought. If it had happened to her, she would want everyone to make a big deal of it — make her feel special.

The voice that she hated whispered in her head.

But it didn't happen to you. Nothing ever happens to you. And it probably never will.

All at once she had a fantasy of the future. Linda, rich, beautiful, famous, seated at the head of a long polished table surrounded by glamorous, glittering, important people. Shelly hovered in the background like a ghost and no one even noticed she was there.

"And it won't cost a cent," her father was saying. "Polli Darnell must have been very impressed."

Shelly snapped out of her black mood.

"What designs did Dean Stoessler send her, Linda?" Shelly made herself ask.

"It must have been the summer collection I did in November. Mr. Frank made me do one of my sketches over. I really should have suspected something then," she said thoughtfully.

"Oh, they were so good," Shelly said sincerely. They really were, she thought. Especially the bathing suits and the matching coverups. So different.

"They *were* good," her mother agreed. "I liked the idea that you had, allowing for various figure faults. It made them very saleable. Not everyone is lucky enough to have a perfect figure. It's nice to think a designer of the future will have us old gals in mind."

"Who says you don't have a great figure, Lou?" Dad said teasingly. "And what's all this about 'old'? Weren't you the one who just told me you liked being forty?"

Her mother smiled at him across the table. "I do, I do," she said quickly. "And I'm glad you approve anyway, dear."

Mrs. Barr turned to Linda again.

"Seriously. The people who design clothes seem to assume that everyone is a size 7 or 8. Five foot ten and absolutely gorgeous. I used to think fashion shows were a kind of special torture for all the women in the bigger sizes, imagining those beautiful clothes on themselves, only to be brought up short by the reality of their own lumps and bumps."

"You don't have that problem, Mom," Linda said. "And I never really thought about doing clothes for the really overweight woman. I'd rather have them look at my clothes and then decide to go on a diet right away."

"That's good," Shelly said, joining the discussion. "The Linda Barr Diet Dress — guaranteed to make you lose fifty pounds."

"Speaking of Linda Barr," her sister said. "Do

you think Linda Leigh sounds better — more professional? Linda Barr — well, doesn't it make you think of a candy bar?" She looked slightly embarrassed.

Shelly stared at her. "Did anyone ever call you that?" she asked.

"Yes," Linda said. "One guy called me Bit O' Honey all through junior high even though I was about a foot taller than he was. Mike Devins just called me 'Sweets' because of the name."

"Paul Sklar called me Fudgie once," Shelly muttered glumly.

"Well, that's sweet too," her mother said, laughing.

"And sometimes nutty," Tony added.

"Oh, you," she said, making a face.

She thought about her sister at Enfield High. When she had been a freshman and then a sophomore, Linda had been a junior and then a senior. She remembered Linda's name appearing on the National Honor Society list but she couldn't remember many girl friends, or for that matter, boyfriends coming to the house. There had been phone calls, Shelly remembered, but it seemed that they usually had something to do with school work. She used to wonder about it and many times had felt sorry for Linda, but after awhile she had decided that her sister preferred it that way. Certainly she had never complained about it, at least not that Shelly ever knew.

The family talked eagerly all through the dinner that her mother had wisely left in the oven during the reading of the letter. Even with all the excitement, Mom still thinks of things like that, Shelly thought.

When Ryan came at seven-thirty they were all still at the table, lingering over their coffee and tea. Linda looked almost shy when Shelly told Ryan the good news.

"Hey, that's really great," he said, his smile wide and his teeth shining in the lamplight. Shelly couldn't tell for sure in the rosy light but she sensed that he was blushing. He *is* scared of her, she thought. He thinks he's not in her class or something. And he was probably right, at least in Linda's own eyes. Her sister would never look at a mere mechanic no matter how talented he was, or how good-looking. The guy she dated now was on his way to being a doctor. The other few dates she had had, Shelly remembered, included a law student and a brilliant chemical engineering student. Another date had been the grandson of a former governor. He had been really boring, Shelly thought now, but Linda had seemed to ignore that fact. Instead she had talked incessantly about his "breeding" and "background."

I'll take Ryan any day, Shelly decided, now looking at him as he chatted with her mother and father. When he smiled he was really outstandingly handsome with his hair and eyes shining and the color high on his cheeks. He had a gorgeous complexion, Shelly thought, not for the first time.

Once she told him "If you were a girl you wouldn't even need blusher."

"Oh, but I do!" he answered straight-faced. "And then sometimes I put too much on and then I look just terrible."

She had thrown a couch pillow at him then and they both laughed.

"Don't make fun of us poor palefaces," she had said.

"Movie starts at eight-twenty," he said now as he watched her get up from the table and start to clear dishes.

"Leave those, Shelly," her mother said. "Linda and Tony can help me. Thorn, how about you giving the twins their bath tonight? Anyway, you and Ryan go along and have a good time."

"Are you going like *that*?" Linda asked her pointedly.

Shelly hadn't planned to change her clothes. She looked fine, she thought. She had planned to wash her face and brush her hair and spray on some of the cologne Ryan liked. She didn't answer her sister.

"Be right down," she told Ryan and ran quickly up the stairs. The pleasure she had felt during dinner vanished.

She thinks I'm a real mess, Shelly thought bitterly. She's probably even ashamed of me. She brushed her long hair listlessly. And she's right, she thought. So far I'm nothing to be very proud of. She fixed her face, not meeting her own eyes in the mirror. She thought of going back downstairs and telling Ryan that she didn't feel good, that she couldn't go to the movies after all and then coming up to her haven and the comfort of the warm quilt and the whale book.

He'd be disappointed, she decided. He works so hard after school. She walked down the stairs slowly and on the last step she stopped for a long moment, took a deep breath, and squared her shoulders. She pasted a big, happy smile on her lips and announced: "Ryan. I'm ready. We can go now."

Chapter 7

Shelly woke up early, instantly aware that today she had to wash, dry, and iron *all* her clothes. It really was disgusting. She didn't have one stitch of clean clothing to put on. In fact, she would have to spend the next few hours in her bathrobe. Happily, on weekends, the Barrs often took their time getting dressed unless there was something special doing. Bathrobes were in! Still, she was glad she wouldn't have to admit the real reason why she wasn't getting dressed this Saturday morning.

She lay in bed, cozy, comfortable, but not really content. The memory of last night filtered through her mind.

It was a disaster! She, close to tears all night, even though the movie was really funny judging by the reaction of the people around them. Ryan too. He laughed madly at the antics onscreen, repeatedly nudging her, wanting her to join in the fun.

She couldn't even smile; she was too depressed. After a while his constant pokes and eager questions, "Did you see that?" or "Did you hear what that guy said?" really began to get on her nerves.

She whispered sharply, "Cut it out, will you?"

His startled expression, the quick flash of hurt on his face filled her with guilt, but she deliberately averted his face.

What does he know? she thought angrily, silent tears causing a giant lump in her throat. He could care less about how I feel tonight. If he really loved me, he wouldn't have taken me to this dumb movie. He would —

"Do you want to leave?" he whispered.

She shook her head "no." She couldn't get up now, walk up the long aisle, face the bright lights of the lobby. Why didn't he leave her alone?

"Shelly."

His voice was very soft and tender, almost like he was talking to a baby. Had he seen the glint of tears in her eyes? He reached for her hand and she let him hold it, but she couldn't squeeze his hand as she usually did. Still, it felt good. Maybe she could tell him. Maybe he would understand how terrible it was to be so ordinary when your sister was so special. And to be so jealous that it made your insides sick. To have half of you love that special sister so much, to be so truly and honestly proud of her, while the other half screamed and raged: *It isn't fair!*

And it wasn't fair. What did her mother and father really think? What was it like for them to have their firstborn daughter so perfect, so remarkable, and then their second daughter so, well, so imperfect and unremarkable? Could she tell Ryan all that without him saying something awful like, "Don't be ridiculous, Shelly," or look at her with pity or disgust in his eyes?

She needed to talk to someone so badly and Ryan

said he loved her. If he really cares, he will understand, she thought. She leaned toward him and managed to choke out: "I want to leave."

He released her hand quickly and stood up. They made their way up the aisle. Ryan led the way and he didn't look back.

He's mad at me, she thought suddenly. He really wanted to see this movie and I spoiled it for him. He's tired and not in the mood to listen to my problems. Who wants a mixed-up wreck for a girl friend anyway?

She remembered now how her spine had stiffened then and how hard she had bitten her lower lip. She wouldn't tell him a thing, she decided. Why should she risk having him think badly of her? She really didn't want *anyone* to know what a terrible person she was. Ryan loved his sister. He would never be able to understand how anyone could have such evil feelings for a member of the family. She would handle it alone, she decided. She would just tell him she felt sick and let him think what he wanted. It served him right anyway. All he really cared about tonight was that stupid movie.

Somewhere inside, she knew she wasn't being quite fair but at least the anger was helping to keep the tears away.

"I want to go right home," she said abruptly as they reached the lobby. "I'm sorry," she said in a voice she knew didn't sound sorry at all.

His blue eyes searched her face for a long moment and then he looked away.

"All right then," he said shortly.

He drove her home without saying another word. When he parked the car in front of her house, she got out quickly, not explaining, not inviting him in.

"Good night," she had mumbled. She knew for sure he was angry then.

This morning the sharpness of her pain had dulled so that now when she thought of it, thought of what she had done to Ryan, she was ashamed. What's the matter with me? Now I'll really have some fast talking to do. I acted like a fool.

I'll just tell him — What would she tell him?

She hopped out of bed and looked around the room for her fluffy slippers. She got down on all fours and looked under the bed. There they were, all the way under, covered with gray dust kitties. Besides doing her laundry, she really should give this room a good cleaning, she thought.

Flat on her stomach, reaching for the elusive slippers, she decided: I'll tell him the truth. I'll call him tonight when he gets home from work and ask him to stop over for a little while. Usually, Ryan spent Saturday evenings with his mother and Kathleen and went to bed early. But if he's over here it will be easier. We'll get all comfortable in the kitchen and we can really have a good talk. It will be easier tonight because I won't be all messed up like I was last night. I'll tell him how upset I was, how confused, and how I was afraid he would think I was awful. He'll put his arms around me right in the kitchen. He'll say, "I understand exactly how you feel, but you're wrong. You *are* special and you're wonderful and — "

Slippers in hand at last, she slid back out from under the bad and lay perfectly relaxed on the floor.

LOCAL GIRL GETS HEAD STRAIGHT
WHILE UNDER BED

She visualized the bold headline and laughed out loud. Tony's right, she thought. I am *nutty*.

The Barr household was a busy place. Everyone was occupied with his or her own chore. Even the twins had been given dust cloths and they were happily slapping at the bookshelves in the living room, jabbering to each other and to anyone who would listen.

Shelly was still in her bathrobe but already she had a feeling of accomplishment. Shirts, slacks, jeans, sweaters, tees were on hangers or in the basket waiting to be put away. I should do this every few days, she thought, and not let myself get down to nothing like I do.

The phone rang and Shelly's first thought was Ryan, but then she realized it couldn't be he. He was working now.

"Linda?" her mother called up the stairs. "It's Howard."

Her sister had been going out with Howard Lund every Saturday night for the past month. Maybe he's calling to break their date, Shelly thought hopefully, and then caught herself. That's really rotten, she said inwardly. How low can you get? She knew Linda liked Howard quite a lot, at least she seemed to light up when he called or when she announced another date with him.

In Shelly's opinion, Howard was unexceptional in the looks department but he had a ready smile and he was always pleasant enough. There was really nothing to dislike, Shelly thought, but nothing to get too excited about either. Maybe Linda went for the quiet, pale types, but Shelly preferred Ryan's energy, his intensity, his cheerfulness. Just looking at him, she thought, you can tell he's deep, and although she had never really seen it, she sensed he had a fierce temper. He had told her he did.

"But don't say it's because I'm Irish. That's like saying every Irishman is a boozer and a poet. I hate lumping people together like that. Lots of people have terrible tempers," he had said, adding, "I don't get mad very often but when I do — " He knit his brow and scowled at her. "Watch out!"

She had laughed. She couldn't imagine Ryan ever getting really mad at her. They got along like peanut butter and jelly.

Now, she just hoped she could explain well enough so he would forgive her for last night.

"What are you doing tonight?" Linda asked, appearing in the doorway.

Shelly looked up from the ironing board, honestly surprised.

"Nothing much," she said. "I have some reading to do for school."

"You're not seeing Ryan?"

"No. Well, I was going to call him. He stays home on Saturday night usually. The weekends are really murder at the garage, he tells me. Everyone and his brother brings his car in and wants a rush job."

Linda looked thoughtful.

"You wouldn't want to go on a double date with me to The Carousel, would you?" she asked.

Shelly's heart leaped. This was a first!

"With Ryan?" She knew he couldn't afford The Carousel.

"Not with Ryan. With Nick Kent, Howard's

cousin from Connecticut. He's a premed student at Stinnett, too, but he's spending this weekend with Howard's family. Howard said his mother insisted that he include Nick in his plans for tonight."

Shelly tried to push down the excitement.

"What is he? A real jerk or something?"

"Not at all," Linda said patiently. "I asked Howard all about him. Of course, we can take it for granted that he comes from an excellent family. He lives in Greenwich and, well, you know that's *very* nice. His father and his grandfather are both well-known surgeons and Nick plans to follow in their footsteps." Linda's voice held more than a trace of awe.

Shelly groaned.

"But Linda, what does he *look* like?"

She could just imagine. Why else would Linda be asking her? If he's gorgeous, she would probably call a classmate. Except, she thought suddenly, Linda has never mentioned the girls at school. Was it possible that Linda really didn't have anyone else to ask? Shelly softened.

"Howard said he's an attractive person. I wouldn't fix you up with anyone repulsive," Linda said defensively.

The idea was exciting again. The Carousel! The restaurant that even her mother and father thought was elegant, if too expensive to visit often. Howard must really be rich.

But what about Ryan? He had never really asked her *not* to go out with anyone else. He had never said it. Shelly had just taken it for granted.

Maybe that was the trouble. She let Ryan take up so much of her time and heart, she probably was missing a lot! No other boy had really appealed to her since Ryan but this Nick did sound interesting.

"Let me think about it," Shelly said, not wanting to appear too eager.

Linda nodded agreeably and turned away.

Shelly knew the real reason for her excitement. This was a chance to show her sister how well she could handle herself, how likeable she was, how —

No, it wasn't that. She didn't feel *that* sure of herself. The real reason was because she wanted Linda to like her, to even admire her, and maybe if she did well tonight, her sister would look at her with new eyes. Maybe tonight they could really be equals.

She just wouldn't mention it to Ryan, that's all. She shouldn't allow him to run her life so completely anyway. Why should she miss out on everything? After all, it would be Saturday night. Ryan might like to go to bed early every single Saturday night of his life, but she didn't. She wanted to go to The Carousel!

"Okay!" Shelly said. "I'll go."

Linda popped back into the pantry and sat on the stool. She was smiling.

"That's great, Shelly." Two creases appeared on her forehead. "What will you wear?" she asked.

"My navy wool?" Shelly suggested tentatively. What *did* you wear to an elegant restaurant?

Linda looked dubious.

"My pantsuit?"

"Something simple but sophisticated," Linda decided. "I know you're only sixteen," she said, "but you don't have to tell the world that. Come on up to my room when you finish and we'll think some more about it."

"Okay," Shelly said casually. Inside, she was seething with excitement. She just knew Linda was going to lend her something to wear. With her sister's help, maybe she would look really good tonight and then all eyes would follow her like they did Linda.

They spent the next two hours in Linda's room going through her closet, her jewelry box, and her makeup drawer. Best of all, when Linda handed her the dusty pink wool skirt and matching sweater, she didn't say one word about taking care of it. Shelly realized it was her sister's way of apologizing for her part in the blouse episode.

The medium-sized gold hoop earrings and the solid bangle bracelet seemed exactly right. When Linda added the small, domed dinner ring, Shelly was in seventh heaven.

"My nails are a mess," Shelly admitted. "And I better wash my hair now so it will be completely dry."

Linda gave her a bright smile.

"I know. Why don't we each take our bath now, do our hair, and then I'll give you a manicure. I have the perfect polish for that outfit."

"That's great!" Shelly said eagerly. She was looking forward to a whole afternoon of beauty routines. It would be something completely new for her but Linda did it all the time and she knew all about it. Maybe she would really learn something. Anyway, she decided, she was just going to relax and enjoy it.

Linda tilted her head to one side and studied Shelly.

"I wonder how you'd look with your hair up?" she said. "I have a new magazine with a section about hair. Let's look through that later, all right?"

"All right!" Shelly breathed. It was so nice having an older sister who knew all the tricks. She should have asked her for advice long before this.

After a long, soaky bath and a good shampoo, Shelly toweled dry and wrapped her hair up turban-style. She cleared the steam from the bathroom mirror and looked at herself.

Her face was pink from the heat, her eyes were clear and bright, and her nose — her mother was right — she really did have a good nose. Why had she hated her face so much? It wasn't bad at all. And why had she neglected herself? Why, it was fun getting ready for a date like this. Already she felt pampered and almost pretty. If Ryan could see her in the pink outfit with her hair done differently —

She put Ryan firmly out of her mind. She wasn't going to think about him. Tonight she was going out with Nick Kent, a Stinnett man!

She knew about Stinnett College. Who didn't? It was small but famous. Either you had to be very smart or very rich to get in, she had heard. For a moment she wondered if this Nick was rich. Linda had implied he was. She knew it was important to her sister but for herself she really didn't know if it mattered.

Anyway, rich or poor, smart or only average, ugly or handsome, she hoped just one thing. That he would like her. It would really be terrible if he didn't. What would Linda think of her then?

Chapter 8

Nick *didn't* like her! She could tell right away. He took one short look during the introductions and then his eyes flicked away. Not in Linda's direction as she would expect but to the mirror over the hall table. He moved slightly closer to it and as they stood, making polite conversation, he watched himself in the glass, moving his head this way and that, smiling as he talked, his eyes never leaving his own face.

Maybe he thought no one knew what he was doing, but Shelly did. She had seen girls in school do the same thing in the girls' room and older women do it in department stores, but this was worse. This was awful! How could he appreciate her when he was so pleased with himself?

"You two look fantastic," Howard said. "We'll have to chase the competition off tonight, right Nick?"

"Oh, right," Nick said, smiling at himself.

A few minutes ago, Shelly had almost floated down the stairs, filled with new confidence. She knew she looked good. It wasn't only the pink outfit or the good jewelry or even the elegant hairdo. It was a feeling of being totally well-groomed, perfectly put together. She just knew she looked her very best.

Now here was this guy who loved himself and it had all been for nothing!

No. Wait a minute. Howard said she looked fantastic, she could tell her parents thought so, and even Linda had flashed her a look of approval. Never mind about this Nick, she still felt good.

In the car he was friendlier, more outgoing, even asking her questions about herself. She answered him, trying to sound enthusiastic, and after a while she began to think maybe she had misjudged him.

He really wasn't very good-looking. In fact, his face was so long and narrow and his forehead so smooth and high that it made her think of a dill pickle. Pickle-face, she thought, and almost laughed out loud.

His dark hair was nice though. Stylishly cut and he had very definite, well-shaped eyebrows over big brown eyes. He wore clothes well too, she noticed. And he *reeked* of aftershave lotion or something. It didn't look like he had to shave yet either.

Maybe Nick's problem was that he didn't like himself *enough* rather than the other way around. Maybe that's why he needs the mirror, she thought. She decided to wait and see. It was wrong to make snap judgements. Why ruin the night before it even began?

"It's beautiful," Shelly whispered to Linda.

The Carousel was even better than she had imagined. The restaurant had atmosphere all right!

It featured a huge rotating circular platform complete with painted horses and poles under a gay canopy. The lighting was dim but cleverly designed to focus on the rich golds and reds. Somehow it didn't look at all gaudy. Instead it gave the impression of grandeur. Quickly, Shelly adjusted her face to look cool and sophisticated. She didn't want to look like a little girl at her first circus, she thought.

A distinguished gray-haired man in a red jacket and black tie led them to a table. As Shelly approached the moving platform, she had a terrifying thought: What if I fall? Almost as if he had read her mind, Nick stepped close to her and put his hand under her elbow, guiding her. Shelly noticed Howard doing the same thing to Linda. Well, one thing, she thought, these guys have manners!

Once they were seated, Shelly tried to think of something to say, to show her pleasure and to start a conversation too.

"This is a *really* nice place," she said, making her voice bright. She lowered her voice. "It must be *very* expensive."

Linda's perfect eyebrows went up and both Howard and Nick looked at each other, then laughed.

Howard's pale eyes smiled at her.

"Don't worry. I don't think we'll have to wash dishes."

"I didn't mean — " Shelly started, flustered. It had been a stupid thing to say. Naturally they had plenty of money. It was just that she always had prices in mind when she went out with Ryan. He worked so hard for his money.

It wasn't that she was so dumb about good restaurants either. Her mother and father had taken them out to dinner many times. With the family, though, she had never had to worry about what to say or how she looked or what she ordered. Her parents insisted on good behavior, but you said anything you wanted and ate whatever you thought was good.

Now looking at the menu, her mind raced. What would be the easiest food to manage? She vetoed both lobster and broiled chicken as too messy and tried to decide between prime ribs or stuffed shrimp. Shrimp won. The roast beef was apt to have lots of gravy and she had to think of the pink outfit. If she spilled anything —

Linda was very quiet, she noticed, but smiled often and Howard seemed pleased with her. Nick kept looking around, his long, narrow fingers restlessly tapping the tabletop.

"I bet you play the piano," Shelly said, desperate to break the silence.

"What?" Nick said.

"The way you're — your fingers — I mean, you *seem* like you might play the piano."

His face looked sad suddenly. "My mother says they're surgeon's hands," he said.

"Your father is, isn't he?"

"The best. I'm supposed to carry on the family tradition." He looked sadder.

"Of course you will, Nick," Linda said, speaking for the first time. "Why wouldn't you?" She looked honestly puzzled.

"Now *you* sound like my mother," Nick said. "She can't imagine my wanting to do anything else. It's always been taken for granted that I would start at Stinnett and then go on to medical school.

My grandfather is a surgeon too. So are two of my uncles. It has been preordained that Nicholas Morrow Kent will be a doctor too." He sounded very bitter, Shelly thought.

"But that's wonderful," Linda said, her eyes glowing. "You'll be doing something great. You'll be an important man."

She turned to Howard. "Both of you. I admire anyone who has the brains and good sense to be a professional. And a doctor is just the — epitome!" Her voice was dramatic.

Shelly was surprised by her sister's unusual display of enthusiasm. She had never seen Linda so awe-stricken. She hadn't realized how impressed her sister was with doctors.

"What would you rather do?" Shelly asked Nick.

"That's the problem," he said gloomily. "I don't know. It would make it easier if I had a burning ambition to be an artist or something. But I don't. The truth is I just don't know. So I guess a surgeon is as good as anything."

Howard looked annoyed for the first time.

"Once you're in the operating room you had better know. You'll be responsible for human lives."

Nick's reply was a short "I know," and any further conversation was cut off by the appearance of a waiter.

Shelly admired Howard's smoothness as he ordered for all of them. He, like Linda, seemed poised and cool. They both had an ease in social situations which made them alike, Shelly thought.

While they waited for dinner, the conversation came to a halt. Nick looked like he had lost all interest in the evening and Linda's face was expressionless. Was her sister always this quiet and removed? It was not like any date Shelly had ever been on. Where was the good-natured teasing, the laughter?

Didn't anyone believe in a good joke, for instance? Shelly racked her brain, trying to think of one. Something was definitely needed to spark up the evening.

"Open your hand, Nick," Shelly said. She would break the ice if it killed her.

He looked at her questioningly but he put his hand out.

"Okay," she said. "Listen, I have a fly in my hand. His name is Irving." She showed him her own closed fist. "I'm going to ask you to hold his hat. Will you?" she said.

He nodded, not smiling.

"Okay, here's his hat and would you mind holding his umbrella, too?" she asked. She pretended to put them in his outstretched hand. She waited about ten seconds.

"Nick, do you *really* believe I have a fly in my hand?"

His voice was bored. "No, I don't."

Shelly burst out laughing. *"Then what are you holding his hat and umbrella for?"* She laughed harder at the look on his face.

She poked Linda. "*Look* at him!" She kept on laughing.

Her sister looked pained. "Shelly! People are looking," she whispered.

Shelly stopped laughing. She felt like Linda had slapped her. Weren't you allowed to laugh at The Carousel? Did sophisticates like Linda and Howard and Nick think jokes were low class or something? Sure, hers had been silly. It was meant to be. Now she felt like a fool. She could feel tears in her eyes. She excused herself and headed blindly for the ladies' room. She just had to get away from all of them.

By the time she located it, she was glad she had decided to make the trip when she did. She hurried through the lovely mirrored outer room to the bathroom beyond. She would just make it. Suddenly, she stopped short. Every booth was locked! She knew without looking that she didn't have a dime in her purse. What was she going to do? There was no one around to ask.

Quickly she lowered herself to the floor and wiggled under the door. Just in time! She heard voices in the outer room. Wouldn't that have been just her luck, she thought. Caught sneaking under the bathroom door at The Carousel?

If Linda ever knew —

Oh, no, Linda's pink sweater and skirt!

She checked herself thoroughly. Thankfully no damage had been done, but she had lost that glamorous feeling.

Her dinner was waiting when she returned to the table. She was glad to have something to do, but she hoped Nick wasn't watching her eat.

"This is delicious," she said once politely.

Linda and Howard were talking in low tones to each other. Shelly couldn't hear a word they were saying.

All at once, Nick became very talkative. He went on and on about a big party he had attended during Christmas vacation. She kept nodding and smiling but it was hard to chew and swallow with his eyes on her. She never thought twice about eating in front of Ryan.

She toyed with her salad. She would never be able to eat it without cutting it first. Really, all it was was a wedge of lettuce with her favorite blue-cheese dressing. She decided to have at least one bite.

When Nick looked away for a moment, Shelly picked up her knife and fork and began to —

Oh, no!

The entire lettuce wedge, dressing and all, catapulted out of the plate and landed in the tray of hot rolls.

Linda's eyes widened and Howard blinked. Nick laughed delightedly for the first time.

"Pretty neat shot," he said.

Shelly wished she could crawl under the tablecloth. Why did things like this happen to her? She couldn't imagine Linda ever being caught without a dime or mucking up the dinner table. She didn't look at her sister. She speared the lettuce with her fork and returned it to her salad plate. She was sure Linda was sorry she had asked her to come along. The feeling was mutual.

"Care to visit The Poet's Corner after this? It's a little place in Cambridge. On Saturday nights they have readings. Some of the stuff is quite good. Linda and I enjoy it," Howard said.

Nick shrugged, a closed look on his face.

It sounds like a quiet place, Shelly thought. My gosh, what would they talk about?

"Let's go where there's music," Shelly said boldly.

Maybe they could dance and the evening could be saved, she thought.

A look of distaste passed over Howard's face but he said, "Fine. If that's what you want." He looked at Linda. "All right with you?" he asked her.

She nodded ever so slightly and Shelly thought of a queen bestowing a royal favor on her lowly subjects. They're both so high and mighty. Taking the kiddies out to play, she thought resentfully.

Nick looked happier, though. Maybe he had enough of this super-boring evening too. If she could use one short word to describe this whole evening it would have to be *dull.* Wouldn't Sandy laugh when she described it to her.

The disco was another world. The music was overwhelming, like so many hammers beating at her brain. After a few minutes, though, she recognized the song and she felt her body begin to react. The strobe lights played crazily over the bodies of the dancers and Shelly watched everything hungrily. Wouldn't her friends love this place? Wait until she told them she had been to The Ground Floor.

There wasn't a chance of being heard in here. No conversation was necessary. Now she could really start to enjoy herself. For a few moments she was content just to stand and watch, soaking up the whole scene like a sponge. Any minute now Nick would lead the way to the dance floor. *Then* she could show him, and her sister, that she wasn't a klutz. She could feel the music. It was part of her now.

Howard's mouth was moving. Above the noise he

was shouting something. She watched him. Finally she made out his words. "We're leaving," he was saying. Without looking back, he and Linda made their way through the crowd. There was nothing to do but follow.

Outside, the sudden silence was a shock. She looked at Howard and Linda. What was the matter?

"Unbelievable," Howard said. "My ears hurt. Sorry, gang — I couldn't stand it."

"I don't like those lights," Linda said. "They made me nauseous."

No one said anything more and Shelly kept her comments to herself. What's the use? she thought.

The Poet's Corner was an arty little coffeehouse in Harvard Square. They listened first to the poems of a painfully thin, frizzle-haired girl. She had the saddest face of anyone Shelly had ever seen. All her poems had something to do with sickness and death. By the time she finished reading, Shelly felt very depressed.

Linda and Howard looked impressed and talked eagerly about the girl's "depth." They seemed to especially like the poems of a tall red-bearded boy with a deep, deep voice. Nick looked bored to tears but he made an effort to be attentive, she noticed, and he smiled a lot — a smile that never seemed to reach his eyes.

Shelly hated the black bitter coffee which was served in tiny cups, but she sipped it bravely. She longed for a *real* cup of coffee loaded with milk and sugar, but she didn't ask.

On the way home, Shelly gave up trying to talk and relaxed against the rich upholstery of Howard's car. What did it matter what Nick thought of her?

He would never ask her out again, anyway. She was sure that he had been just as bored with her as she had been with him. Linda could have this so-called sophisticated life; she would rather have —

Nick's arm was around her shoulder suddenly and he was pulling her toward him. Before she could think, he was kissing her, his lips cold and hard against hers. She let him kiss her for a few seconds until she couldn't stand it anymore. She pulled away. Why, his kiss seemed almost angry. Certainly his lips weren't soft and sweet like Ryan's.

She shuddered inwardly and moved away from him, turning her face to look out the car window. She could feel his eyes on her for a minute. She heard him sigh and she relaxed. She didn't think he would try that again.

Let him think she was a jerk. She just didn't like him that much, she decided. If he meant the kiss as a compliment, fine. She wouldn't be mad or anything. Funny though, his hard kiss hadn't *felt* complimentary. In fact, her lips still hurt where he had pressed them against her teeth. Suddenly, it was funny. Here was this wealthy Stinnett man, a so-called sophisticate, and he didn't even know how to kiss. She looked at her sister sitting primly in the front seat of the car. She wondered if Linda knew what a real kiss was like. A real kiss — the kind Ryan knew how to give. Suddenly, she missed him with all her heart.

Chapter 9

At breakfast, Shelly heard about it from Tony. His voice was accusing, and no wonder, she thought. He considered Ryan his best friend.

"I really felt sorry for him," he said. "He comes over to surprise you and what happens? *His* girl is out with another guy. Didn't you even tell him, Shel?"

"Well, no," she admitted. "It all happened so fast."

She tried to defend herself. "He never comes on Saturday night. Besides, what's wrong with my dating someone else? We're not engaged or anything."

Tony shot her a look. "Oh, yeah? Would you like it if he took someone else out? Wouldn't you be bent out of shape?" He answered for her. "You would. I know you would."

"Was he really mad?" Shelly asked in a small voice.

"Mad? Sure. But Shel, he's more hurt than anything else. If you could have seen the look on his face when Mom told him where you were." Tony shook his head grimly.

She felt terrible. She should have at least warned Ryan — not let him hear it from someone else. The worst thing about the whole thing was that it hadn't been worth it. Not a bit. She didn't even have a good time. Ryan was a hundred times nicer than Nick; she knew that now. He was cuter, more fun to be with, and he really cared for her. Or at least he had. What would he say to her?

She glanced at the kitchen clock. It was ten thirty-five. She had to call him. Maybe after a good night's sleep he wasn't mad anymore.

She went to the phone in the hall. The little alcove with the table and comfortable chair was almost like a separate room, giving her quiet and privacy. The twins were playing in the living room and she was glad they weren't around her. She needed all her wits about her to make this call.

"Ryan? It's Shelly." She waited.

His hello had been pleasant enough but his reaction to her voice was a surly grunt.

"I didn't wake you up, did I? I mean, it's Sunday and I know you all like to sleep late. Me too. I mean, I like to sleep late on Sundays too." She stopped. She knew she was babbling.

"I was up," Ryan said.

She decided to get right to it.

"Ryan, about last night. Linda asked me to go just yesterday. Her boyfriend's cousin was visiting and, well, it was a favor. It didn't mean anything, really. It wasn't even fun!" She knew her voice was too high and she was talking too fast.

"How come you came over last night anyway?"

She decided to change her tack. She hated having to defend herself.

His voice was low — very quiet.

"Mom and Kathleen went visiting. I decided not to go. I wanted to see you."

Her heart sank.

"Why didn't you call earlier? How could I know? You *never* come over on Saturday." Even to herself, she sounded terrible.

"It doesn't matter now," he said. "I get the message. You don't want to be my girl, that's all."

His voice was so full of sadness that she suddenly felt impatient.

"Oh, for heaven's sake, Ryan. It doesn't mean that at all. Anyway, we never said we couldn't date other people. I mean, we don't *own* each other."

"That's true," he said in that strange, quiet voice. "I don't own you."

"And if something comes up, then we should be able to understand without getting mad about it. I mean, you have to realize that — "

"I understand," Ryan said, his voice loud. "I understand perfectly. You'd rather go out with some college guy. Someone who can take you to snazzy restaurants. I understand *that*, all right."

"Oh, Ryan," she said. "That's not true — "

"Listen, Shelly. Let's not drag it out anymore. Let's just say I've been holding you back. From now on, I won't get in your way. You're free to do what you want."

"But I want — "

"Awww — you don't know what you want, Shelly," he said disgustedly. "All I know is I'm through."

"Ryan!" she wailed. He couldn't do this.

"Ryan?" she said again. There was a click and after a few seconds she realized there was no one on the line. He had hung up on her!

She was mortified. She was indignant. She felt the heat rise in her face. How could he talk to her like that? What right did he have to treat her like that? How could he be so hard? So cruel?

She sat with one hand on the phone, not moving, frozen, really, her mind reeling with shock. Suddenly, she realized her mother was beside her, saying something. She forced herself to listen. She saw the concern on her mother's face and felt the sympathy in the arm around her shoulder and in the tone of her voice.

"What happened, honey? What did he say?"

"He — he broke up with me," she told her.

She couldn't say anymore. She felt her fact start to crumple. It hurt so much inside. Was this the same way Ryan had felt? Had she done this to him? She couldn't bear it.

She couldn't stay here in the hall either. Any minute she would cry and she had to get away. Her mother was so good but even she couldn't help now. No one could. She stood up and ducked out of the circle of her mother's arm.

"Excuse me, Mom," she choked out and ran up the stairs.

Not until she reached her own room and shut the door did she allow the tears to spill over. She threw herself across the unmade bed and buried her hot face in the quilt.

Ryan. She thought his name over and over as the sobs tore from her throat. She had never felt so terrible. Her throat ached and her head hurt. It was worse than anything she had ever experienced. Even her chest hurt. For the first time, she knew what the expression "broken heart" meant. Just now, Ryan Gallagher had broken her heart. And what was worse, she knew she had broken his, too.

There was nothing she could do about it. She cried into the quilt until there were no tears left. When she quieted, she crawled under the covers and pulled them over her head. She knew she couldn't face anyone now. She just wanted to stay here, all curled up, and forget everything. What was that song? "Make The World Go Away"? Yes, that's what she wanted. She felt so cold and shivery and alone. No one could ever understand how she felt — no one. She pulled her knees up tight against her chest. She fell asleep that way just before noon on that clear and sunny Sunday.

At four-thirty, when shadows had crept into the corners of her room, Shelly woke up. For a few moments, still cradled in the soft hands of sleep, she didn't remember a thing. Then the memory of the morning came back to her. She didn't feel like crying again, though, and when a knock came at her door, her eyes were clear and dry.

It was her father.

"Open the door for me, Shel. My hands are full," he said.

She hopped out of bed quickly and let him in. He was carrying a tray, the old white wicker one with legs that had been in the family for years. Whenever she had been sick in bed, that tray was hers for meals and play.

"Get back in bed so I can set this thing down."

Shelly saw roast beef, peas, mashed potatoes, gravy, just the way she liked it. She spotted another bowl covered with a napkin.

"What's this?" she asked, then peeked.

It was tapioca, warm and fluffy the way her grandmother used to make it especially for her. It was her favorite food. She was touched.

"Who made it?" she asked.

"Linda did. She thought it would make you feel better," her father said.

"I'm all right now," Shelly said quietly.

"I can see that," her father said. "Mind if I sit for a few minutes? At my age I can use a little rest now and then."

"At *your* age!" Shelly snorted.

Thornton Barr had steel gray hair but his skin was smooth and youthful and his eyes were bright and blue and alive. Now his eyes studied her seriously.

"Rough day, huh?" he asked.

Shelly talked between bites. Suddenly she was starved!

"I guess Mom told you Ryan broke up with me," she said.

He nodded. "Did you ever agree not to go out with anyone else?"

She shook her head. "We really didn't. I mean, we never actually said that. But I guess if I have to be honest, we both *assumed* it. I should have known he'd be mad."

"Mad or hurt?" her father asked.

"Both. He's through with me."

"Ryan always struck me as a person with a lot of pride," her father said thoughtfully.

"Oh, he is," Shelly agreed. "He can't stand to be made a fool of."

"Who can?" her father said. "And no one likes to feel guilty either. Or rejected, like you do. You've got to remember, Shel, you didn't set out to hurt him."

"No, I didn't. But I didn't let myself think too hard about his feelings. I just went ahead and did what I wanted to do. Except — you know what? I had a lousy time."

Her father touched her hair. "Listen, sweetheart, it may be quite a while before Ryan gets over this, and if you care about him, you're going to have to be patient. I could say forget about him, that there are plenty of other fish in the sea, but I won't. I won't say you're only sixteen and you're too young to settle for one person. I *could* say those things, but I won't. However — "

"What?" Shelly asked.

"I do have a suggestion."

"I need one. What is it?"

She finished the tapioca, scraping the bowl to get the last few particles. She leaned back on the pillows, waiting.

"Well, right away you should throw yourself into something else. Use all your energies on something new. I'm not talking about a new boyfriend now. What I mean is something that interests you, stimulates your mind. It will help the time pass and whatever you accomplish will give you a good feeling."

"Mmmmm," Shelly murmured, thinking.

"I can't tell you *what* to choose but I trust you to think of something. You have a good mind.

Maybe now it's time to give some serious thought to what you want to do with your life."

He took her hand and held it between his own.

"Remember, Shelly, I'm not pushing — just suggesting. I don't like to see you unhappy." He bent over and kissed her forehead.

He got up and retrieved the tray from her lap and she saw his bright-blue eyes twinkle.

"Although I must say, all this hasn't affected your appetite any," he said.

She couldn't help it; she burst out laughing. So did he. For a moment, Shelly felt that everything was right again. At least she was sure her mother and father really loved her. Even Linda had thought enough of her to make her favorite dessert. All in all, it could be worse.

She felt outrageously lazy and she didn't feel like getting out of bed. Maybe in a little while she would take a nice long bath, put on clean pajamas, and join the rest of the family. She thought of the twins. She had neglected them yesterday. Usually on Saturdays she spent a lot of time with them, playing inside and taking them for a ride in their double stroller. Maybe she should go down now and help her mother with them, bathe them, get them ready for bed. She didn't move. Instead she thought about what her father had said.

"Think about what you want to do with your life."

She remembered Nick saying last night how it would be easier if he had some sort of burning ambition.

She didn't. Not anything definite, anyway. Just a

vague idea of doing something to help people, to make them feel better, and to improve their lives. But unlike Linda or many of her friends, she hadn't decided on a career.

Mom said she had a wonderful way with children. She called it "a gift." But a career involving children wasn't really very glamorous, was it? Not like a fashion designer. Not like, say, a doctor.

A doctor. She remembered the look of reverence on her sister's face when Nick had talked about his plans. It was obvious Linda was impressed and thought the profession was something to be admired. She wondered, suppose I was a doctor? The very first doctor in the Barr family. She cuddled up in her quilt and let the fantasy develop.

She saw herself striding down the hospital corridor, immaculate white coat unbuttoned, a stethoscope hanging from her neck. Her hair was up in a neat but sophisticated twist. As she walked, young nurses and interns spoke to her with respect in their voices.

She entered a private room where Linda lay propped up in bed, her face pale and wan. Her parents, their faces anxious, sighed with relief when they saw Shelly.

"Oh, thank heavens you're here," they said.

Linda had tears in her eyes. "I feel so much better now that I see you. When will you operate?"

"Early tomorrow morning," Shelly said with her usual air of authority. "And don't worry about a thing. I haven't lost a patient yet."

Shelly enjoyed the brief fantasy thoroughly, but suddenly she thought seriously: *Why not? I would be doing something I want to do — making people feel better.* She had never considered the idea before, had never even thought about fooling around with anyone's insides, or actually being responsible for someone's life — but couldn't she learn all that? Sure she could. You can get used to anything, she thought.

Why not? She kept thinking that as the idea took a firm hold. But she wouldn't say a word to anyone in the family yet. But tomorrow she would make an appointment with her guidance counselor and map out the necessary courses for next year. She wished now she had talked more to Nick about Stinnett and had asked about the premed program. It *had* to be Stinnett. Stinnett would definitely sound very impressive.

This then would be her new goal, something to work for, something to put her heart and soul into. This would be the new accomplishment her father spoke of.

So what if Ryan was being difficult? If he wanted to act like that, it was his choice. Anyway, it was probably all for the best, now that she thought about it. The years ahead would be crammed with effort and new experiences. She couldn't afford the time now for boys, even Ryan.

Shelly Barr, M.D. It sounded great. Even better than Linda Leigh, Fashion Designer. After all, the fashion world was really a rather shallow one. A doctor — now that was an important title. She couldn't wait for tomorrow to start the ball rolling.

Her father was right, she thought. I really do have a good brain. And now I'll really have a chance to use it.

Chapter 10

After first period on Monday, she stopped at the guidance office to make an appointment. She was in luck! Mrs. Marcello was free and she would see her right now.

"I was going to schedule you for this month anyway, Shelly. This way, I'm just that much ahead," she said pleasantly.

Shelly found herself sitting up very straight. Something about this woman makes you want to look extra sharp, she thought. Maybe it was her appearance. Springy dark hair cut very short, piercing dark eyes, and a nose that should have been ugly but wasn't. She always wore crisp blouses and tailored suits. She had a no-nonsense look about her, almost stern, but Shelly knew from experience that she was kind. She always made you feel like she was really interested.

Mrs. Marcello searched in her file for Shelly's folder, found it, and sat down again.

"Now. What's on your mind?" she asked.

Shelly plunged right in. "I've decided to study

medicine. I mean, I want to be a doctor. What courses will I need in my senior year?"

If Mrs. Marcello was surprised, she didn't show it.

"When did you decide this, Shelly?" she asked.

"Oh, I've had it in mind for quite a while," she answered quickly. What would she think if she knew she had thought of it only last night?

The counselor didn't say anything; instead she seemed to be waiting for Shelly to continue.

"I guess it started with biology," she improvised. "We had to dissect frogs and worms and stuff and I — uh — enjoyed it very much."

She amazed herself with the easy lie. Actually the experiments had been especially difficult for her. Not that the smell had bothered her as it had so many of the other students, but it had been the cutting — cutting and destroying something that had once been alive and moving. Fine doctor I'll make, she thought.

Mrs. Marcello still seemed to be waiting.

"I've always wanted to be of service to people. And I love science," Shelly added.

"Science and chemistry, in particular, haven't seemed to be your strong subjects, though," Mrs. Marcello said softly, consulting the folder.

"Well, I really haven't done my best," Shelly admitted, relieved to be speaking the truth. "I didn't actually have a set goal, so I guess I have goofed off a lot. It's different now. Now I really want to do well."

Mrs. Marcello smiled. "You'll really have to apply yourself now and next year, that's for sure. Do you have any idea where you want to apply?"

"Stinnett," Shelly said without hesitation.

The counselor's dark eyebrows went up, but she said mildly, "They do have the best premed program in the East. They'll look for A's, though, maybe a few B's. Nothing below that, Shelly."

She flipped through the papers in the folder.

"Luckily, your courses up until now fill the bill. Next year you'll have a heavy load. Let me check."

She left the office for a few minutes and returned with a Stinnett catalog. She turned a few pages and jotted down some notes. "Okay," she said. "Here's next year's requirements." She listed the courses, one at a time: "Physics. One semester each of trig and calculus. I encourage Latin. You're in third year French now, right? Additional English, probably composition. One semester each of sociology and psychology. If you want, you can continue art as your elective. That's it. Think you can handle it?"

Shelly nodded, smiling like mad. Calculus? Physics?

"I should say, your marks this term will count heavily since you'll be applying in the middle of next year. How do you think you're doing now?" Mrs. Marcello asked.

"Pretty well, I think," Shelly said, smiling hard. Starting today she would make sure her final marks would be good, even if it meant nonstop studying.

"Fine, then. I'll make out your schedule accordingly." She leaned back in her chair. "Perhaps your decision came just in time. Now you can make your time here really count. So many students graduate without any idea of what they want for themselves. It's common, of course." She laughed. "You'd be surprised at how many forty- and fifty-year-olds still don't know what they want to do when they grow up."

Before she left the office, Mrs. Marcello wrote out a pass to get her into second period. Shelly thanked her and walked away with her shoulders back and her stomach held in. It wasn't until she was halfway down the hall that she let herself relax and walk normally. When she did that, she felt the doubts creep into her mind again.

Calculus? Latin? Four years of Stinnett, medical school after that, and more years after that of residency training? Ten years or more?

What if she couldn't do it? What if she just wasn't smart enough? It would be terrible if she told the world about it and then failed. Maybe it would be better not to say anything to anybody. Keep her plans completely secret, work hard, and get accepted at Stinnett.

She pictured the joyous family scene when *that* letter arrived. She went into math class, her spirits restored.

But by the end of the period, she was grumbling along with everyone else. Either Mr. O'Connor had decided to change his teaching methods or he had had a big fight with his wife that morning. Or something! He assigned three pages of problems due tomorrow. Usually his homework assignments were light and many times he allowed the work to be done right in class. He was in a bad mood all right. He didn't even crack a smile when Susan Spencer pretended to cry.

On her way to third period, she spotted Ryan coming toward her. He stood out in the crowd, head and shoulders above the two boys he was walking with. Her eyes took in his blonde hair and her favorite shirt — a dark green with an open neck. Whenever he wore that shirt, his blue eyes looked green and catlike.

She paid little attention to what Sandy and Donna were saying. Inside, she was readying herself for the moment when he approached. She was aware that her heart was thudding in her chest.

He was almost here. In just a second they would meet. What would he say? What would *she* say? Ryan was not so stubborn or so mean that he wouldn't —

He passed her! Without a word! His blue-green eyes had flicked over her face without a sign of recognition. He hadn't missed a step! His face hadn't shown any confusion or hesitation; it was as if she simply didn't exist.

The impact of his rejection hit her like a fist in the stomach. It was the same feeling she had when she fell out of the oak tree in the back yard when she was eight or when she belly-flopped off the raft that summer in Maine. She felt like all the wind had been knocked out of her.

She should have expected it. Hadn't he said — just yesterday — I'm through with you? But how could he be so cruel? Why, she always thought Ryan didn't have a mean bone in his body. He loved kids and animals and people and he cried at sad movies. He always had sympathy for people in trouble, always rooted for the underdog.

But she had to face it. Ryan wasn't cruel — he was indifferent!

That was worse, having him just stop caring. She

felt flushed and humiliated. She didn't want to look at anyone.

Sandy and Donna were looking at her.

"What's going on, Shel?" Sandy said in a shocked whisper. Her eyebrows were raised so high they had disappeared under her bangs.

"Yeah," Donna breathed. "What's happening?"

Shelly trusted Sandy with her life but Donna had mouth trouble sometimes. It would be all over school that Shelly and Ryan had broken up. She would look like a fool. Everyone would know she'd been dumped. Well, she wouldn't let that happen.

She squared her shoulders and tossed her head. "Ryan has a problem, I guess," she said flippantly.

"Yeah?" Donna questioned avidly. "What kind of problem?"

Sandy just looked at her seriously.

"Well, I went out with this guy from Stinnett this weekend. Double-dated with my sister. Went to The Carousel, The Ground Floor — really had a super time. Anyway, now Ryan's all upset about it. Like I said, he's got a problem."

Sandy shook her head as if trying to deny what Shelly had said. "Hey," she said. "You and Ryan were going together. I mean, *together*. He didn't even look at anyone else. How come you did that to him?"

Shelly felt a flash of anger. She hated being backed into a corner like this. It made her voice arrogant and her words mean.

"Sandy, *you'd* jump at the chance and you know it."

Sandy ducked her head as if she had been hit. Shelly knew her words had stung. Sandy didn't have many dates. No one asked her. Her friend didn't say another word and immediately Shelly was sorry. She had never wanted to hurt Sandy for any reason. She tried to explain, to cover up her words.

"I mean, Ryan never takes me out on Saturday. Friday is our night. So when Linda asked me to go as a favor to her, I didn't think it would matter. It really was a favor. It was Linda's boyfriend's cousin and — "

Donna broke in eagerly. "You really went to The Ground Floor? What was it like?"

"Super," Shelly said. "Really super."

She was glad when they reached Miss Abbott's room just as the bell rang. She wouldn't have to talk anymore. They split up and headed for empty seats.

Janet Abbott was perched on a table and she waited for the class to settle down before she spoke. She looks especially pretty today, Shelly thought. Red is her color.

For a quick moment, Shelly considered lingering after class was over and talking to her teacher. She was so pretty and smart and she would probably know just how to handle men. If she could just let her hair down with *someone*, get all the things that were bothering her out in the open, maybe then —

"You're all aware that your papers must be in this Friday," Miss Abbott began. "From what I've heard, many of you have really enjoyed this assignment. The feedback I've had makes me think you all consider it more than just required work. Once you really got into the research and reading, well, it seems like you really put your hearts into it.

"So many of you have chosen such interesting subjects. I love Leo's, for instance." She looked directly at the burly wrestler. "He's doing famous left-handed people. And Ginny. She's doing ESP in animals. Shelly has an interesting subject too, one she really cares about — saving whales from extinction." She smiled at Shelly.

"You see what I mean, class?" she continued. "You're not just doing any old thing just to get by. I'm really pleased that you're all really into it and are getting something out of it. I think it's because you chose subjects that mean something to you personally. That's the point, you know. It's not just the technical skills, like learning to write a bibliography."

Shelly had listened intently, carried away by her teacher's enthusiasm, but the minute she finished speaking and went on to other things, she felt panic begin to grow in her. It was Monday and she wasn't anywhere near finished with her research. She still had a whole book to read and another source to find before she could even start writing. She wouldn't have time to make the trip to the Boston Public Library as she planned; the Enfield branch would have to do. Maybe some short magazine article would do the trick; that is, if she could find one.

She wished Miss Abbott hadn't singled her out just now, making it seem like Shelly was ready with something really outstanding. As it stood now, she would be lucky to get it done, period. Still, she had to try to make it good. Hadn't Mrs. Marcello said it was important to get good marks this semester? Miss Abbott had said this paper would count for half of their mark. She felt a heavy weight settle on her shoulders. So much to do. But no matter what, she was going to have to work. Nothing would interfere. Not when so much depended on it. Not when her whole future as a doctor was at stake.

Shelly Barr, M.D., she thought again.

Shelly Gallagher. The name popped into her mind, but as soon as it did, she squelched it firmly.

It'll take ten years to become a doctor, she thought. By that time, I'll barely remember a boy named Ryan Gallagher. So what if right this minute she could picture his face clearly in her mind. It doesn't matter, she thought. He doesn't matter at all.

Chapter 11

Riding home with Sandy on the bus, Shelly tried to be extra nice. She told her about crawling under the bathroom door at The Carousel, making the story as funny as she could until, at last, Sandy laughed. When she told her about the salad flying into the hot rolls, Sandy had a fit and Shelly knew that she was forgiven. She was truly sorry she had snipped at Sandy. After all, she was the best friend she had in the world.

Time was important now too. Walking up the hill to her house, she vowed to make good use of it for the next few days. Every minute must count. She would do her algebra first today. If she really worked at it, she could get it done before supper. The evening would be free for reading.

"Sheddy's home."

Angela's voice was ecstatic. Shelly stood still while the babies hugged her legs.

"Play with Angie?" her sister begged.

Eric said nothing but he stared up at her with big soulful eyes.

She was torn. She had to get to those math problems, but it was true — she hadn't paid any attention to the twins for so long now. They were too little to understand that she had other things to do.

Her mother blew her a kiss from the kitchen doorway.

"Shelly, I didn't say anything to them yet but it's such a gorgeous day. Feel like taking them for a r-i-d-e?" She spelled out the word but Shelly noticed Angela's eyes suddenly sparkle. She sure is a smart cookie, Shelly thought.

Her mother would understand if she said she had a lot of homework, there was no question about that, but — She melted completely at the sight of the twins looking at her so expectantly.

"Want to go for a ride in the stroller?" she asked them. "Just for a little while?" She would compromise, she thought. Just a short ride for them and then she would go straight to her room. No matter what, she thought, I'll get it all done.

Her mother smiled at her. "The fresh air will be good for them. I did take them grocery shopping with me this morning but you know what that is. Just in and out of the car and in the store all the time."

Shelly laughed. "What did Miss Personality-Plus do in the supermarket today?" With strangers, Angela was far from shy and Shelly knew from experience her little sister could come out with some embarrassing comments.

Louise Barr made a face. "She didn't *say* anything but the man in line behind us was bald. I mean a real bowling-ball bald. Anyway, he was leaning over his basket and our little friend here suddenly reached out and rubbed his head." Her mother laughed, remembering. "You should have seen his face."

While her mother was putting heavy jackets and matching hats on the twins, Shelly grabbed a handful of cookies and put them in a plastic bag. She had a momentary twinge of guilt. She should have stuck to her guns and gone straight to her room, but, she thought with a pang, *all* my evenings will be free now. Ryan won't be coming over anymore.

It would be so strange not having him around. Tony would miss him too. What would she do with all the new free time? How would she fill up the empty space?

Study! Read, do extra work for extra credit. Remember, you've got to get A's and B's, she reminded herself firmly.

It's a blessing in disguise, Shelly decided on the way to the garage to get the stroller. If this hadn't happened, if she hadn't gone out with Nick, if Ryan hadn't broken up with her, she would never have made the decision to be a doctor. That was what was important, she thought. My career. What did it matter if her knowledge of the field consisted of just her own visits to Dr. Maltz, their family doctor, and what she saw on TV. She had vague visions of hypodermic needles and tongue depressors, along with vitamins and antibiotics. Well, she would learn. Starting right away. When she went to the library tomorrow, she would look for a book about medicine.

The twins were waiting for her at the front door. They squealed when they saw their stroller and hurried toward her. She laughed as they climbed in, Angela, as usual, struggling to be first. They looked so chubby and cute in their red corduroy jackets and hats. Her mother had put heavy sweaters on underneath, which accounted for the bulky look. She tucked the red plaid wool blanket around their legs and gave them each a cookie.

"Hold on," she said. "Here we go now."

They loved to go fast down the hill. Sometimes she did it twice even though it meant pushing the stroller up the steep incline.

She breathed the cold, crisp air deeply. She was glad she had decided to come out with the twins. Their happy little faces were all the thanks she needed. Algebra can wait a while, she thought. It's my best subject anyway. I'll get it done in no time.

She ran with the carriage firmly in hand. "Wheeee," she yelled as she guided it down the hill.

"Good girl, Sheddy. Good, good girl," Angela yelled.

It was almost seven-thirty before Shelly managed to be alone in her room, and she had the distinct, unpleasant feeling that she had goofed again.

Somehow, she had let the whole afternoon get away from her. After the walk, which had taken them all the way down to the river's edge, Shelly was tired and allowed herself the mindless joy of watching a cartoon on TV with the kids. It was so warm and comfortable lying on the couch in front of the fire that she dozed, only half aware that the twins were sitting on her back. When she heard her mother calling everyone to dinner, she came fully aware with a start, feelings of guilt and self-disgust hitting her hard.

Stupid, she screamed silently. You're so stupid.

You can't do anything you say you'll do. Now you're really behind.

After dinner, with the dishes staring her in the face and the twins clamoring for her attention, Shelly felt the pressure build almost to the boiling point. In desperation, she appealed to her mother.

"May I be excused from everything tonight? I have tons of homework. I'm never going to get it all done."

Her mother looked at her hard. "Shelly, why didn't you tell me? You should have said something earlier. I wouldn't have suggested the walk."

"That's okay," Shelly mumbled.

"You look so tired now, though," her mother said. "Are you sure you'll manage?"

"I'll manage," she said grimly. To herself she said, *I better!*

In her room, sitting at what once had been her grandmother's desk, she felt overwhelmingly tired. Suddenly everything seemed too much. Only four more days before she had to turn in her whale paper, and she hadn't even started. And Ryan didn't care; he didn't love her anymore. Life was horrible. She fought the impulse to put her head down on the desk and cry. It would be so easy to. She felt the tears waiting. Instead she opened her math book and picked up her pencil. She'd get it done even if it killed her. And it probably would, she thought.

She scanned the three assigned pages. Twenty-four problems to a page. She could gladly strangle Mr. O'Connor. What had he been thinking of? This was going to take all night.

She was halfway through the first page when Tony yelled up the stairs.

"Shelly. Phone."

Tony must have the loudest voice in the world, she thought as she went to the top of the stairs.

"Who is it?" she yelled, half-annoyed, half-hopeful. Could it be Ryan?

"It's that college guy," Tony said scornfully. "Nick Kent."

Tony and Ryan could be twins, Shelly thought. They even think alike. She took her time getting to the phone. Why would he be calling? She had figured she would never see or hear from him again.

"Hi, Shelly," he said pleasantly. "How're you doing?"

"Fine. How are you?" Shelly said politely.

"Did you have a good time Saturday night?" he asked.

"Oh, sure," Shelly lied. "It was super."

"Good. Because I'd like to see you again."

"You would?" Immediately she felt stupid, but it was how she felt. It came as a big surprise that Nick found her interesting enough to ask her out again.

"I mean — when?"

She hadn't meant to ask that either. It sounded too eager, as if she really wanted to go out with him.

"Friday night. A party at one of the houses at Stinnett. Very informal, just a get-together. A lot of good guys and gals though. It should be a lot livelier than that coffeehouse." He laughed. "I don't know about you but poetry isn't my bag."

"I like some," Shelly said, thinking of her grandmother. "But a lot of it I don't. Maybe it's because I don't really understand it," she said honestly.

"I figured you liked The Ground Floor better.

The party should be more like that. Music — dance if you want. Will you come?"

Shelly hesitated. Why had she been so friendly during this conversation? It made it more difficult to say no. She didn't really want to go out with Nick Kent again. She didn't have anything against him, unless you wanted to count that awful kiss. It was just that they hadn't clicked. There was no magic like there was with Ryan, no melting feeling around her heart when she heard his voice or caught his smile. But there was no Ryan now. No more Friday night dates. This Friday she would sit home and the phone wouldn't ring unless she —

"Okay," she said, "what time?"

"I'll pick you up about seven-thirty. How's that?"

"Fine," she said and remembered to add, "thanks."

"Thank *you*," he said. "I'll see you then."

"Bye," she said and hung up.

She hated herself. Why had she ever said yes? She didn't even like Nick. Now she had committed herself to spending another whole evening with him. What if he tried to kiss her again? She realized she didn't even have his phone number and there was no way she could call back and tell him she had changed her mind. Now she *had* to go Friday night.

Tony came out of the kitchen into the hall, a stalk of celery in his hand.

"What did he want?" he demanded, waving the celery like a sword. "Hasn't he made enough trouble around here?"

"He hasn't," Shelly said. "It wasn't his fault." She wondered why she was defending him.

"I hate guys who move in like that," Tony said.

"He has to be a real jerk." He crunched into the celery angrily.

"He didn't move in," Shelly argued. "He doesn't even know about Ryan."

"Yeah? Well, I hope you told him. I don't like him anyway. He's stuck on himself."

"He is not!" Shelly said hotly, remembering Nick's mirror romance. "And I'm going out with him Friday night."

"You're nuts," Tony said. "You're really crazy. Now Ryan will really be mad." He glowered. "And he was going to help me modify that engine."

"That's all you care about," Shelly said. "You don't care about him or me. All you care about is him helping you with your ridiculous machines."

"That's a lie," Tony yelled. "Ryan's my friend. *I* wouldn't treat him like dirt the way you did."

"I didn't. If he wants to be unreasonable — "

"*Unreasonable!*" Tony fairly screamed the word.

Mrs. Barr raced in from the living room and Mr. Barr opened the door of his study.

"What is going on here?" he demanded.

"Your daughter is going out with that jerk again," Tony said sullenly.

"Who are you speaking of, Tony?" his father asked quietly now.

"That Nick guy."

"Shelly's choice of dates isn't really any of your business, is it?"

"Well-ll, no. It's just that — "

"Okay. Leave her alone then. I don't want any more loud voices."

Mrs. Barr looked at Shelly. "You're going?" She frowned. "I'm surprised. You didn't seem too enthused about him."

Shelly shrugged, hating to explain it to someone else when she couldn't even explain it to herself.

"It's a date," she said flatly.

"I don't think accepting an invitation just for the sake of having a date is a very good reason," her father said.

"Not if you really don't like him," her mother added.

"I didn't say I didn't like him. He's okay, really. He's taking me to a party at Stinnett," she said.

"I don't know about that," her father said doubtfully. "I remember college parties."

Linda's voice cut in suddenly. Shelly hadn't even noticed her standing there.

"Nick Kent is a very nice guy. He comes from a good family and he's going to be a surgeon," she said, her voice firm and sure. She looked at Shelly. "He was a perfect gentleman Saturday night, wasn't he?"

"Yes," Shelly said meekly, thinking again of that horrible kiss. Why couldn't she get that out of her mind?

She wondered why her sister was standing up for her. Maybe just because Nick was Howard's cousin, and if he looked bad it was a reflection on her taste.

It came to her suddenly. Linda really was hung up on doctors. A doctor, or even someone with intentions of becoming one, was a truly worthy person in her eyes. Wouldn't Linda be surprised when she found out about Shelly's career plans?

Tony sidled back into the kitchen, chomping viciously on his celery. Her father shook his head at everyone in general and went back into his study. Mom gave Shelly one last doubtful look and returned to the living room.

"Thanks, Linda," Shelly said.

Linda smiled. "He must really like you." She looked at Shelly approvingly. "He'll probably take you to a lot of nice places." Shelly marveled that Linda really thought that nice places, good families, and the right clothes were so important.

Linda seemed to read her mind.

"I know I just hate shabby places."

Shelly didn't answer. She couldn't unless she wanted to get into another argument. It was obvious that Linda was referring to her dates with Ryan. She was sure Linda considered movies and hamburger joints "shabby" places.

She kept her mouth shut and went upstairs. By shutting out every thought and concentrating very hard, she had finished the seventy-two problems by eleven-fifteen. She closed the book, took off her clothes, threw an old flannel nightgown over her head, and fell into bed. She completely forgot about the blue book on the bedside table.

Chapter 12

On Wednesday she read the entire book. It took her from four in the afternoon until ten o'clock at night. She took notes as she went along but found when she finished that she had forgotten to number the index cards. They were in a complete mishmash all over her bed and she eyed them with dismay. Tomorrow she would have to get them in order so she could write the paper. It had to be good. No, it had to be more than that. Her final mark depended on it.

She allowed herself to go downstairs for a late snack. Her father made a remark about her becoming a "hermit" but her mother shushed him. Linda stays in her room most of the time, Shelly thought, and he never says anything about that. I guess it's because I'm usually around. I like to be with people. I'm not cut out for the solitary life. Good thing I didn't decide to become a poet or something, she decided.

"Absence makes the heart grow fonder," she said teasingly, adding, "and familiarity breeds contempt."

"Listen to her," her father said, laughing. "Just full of old saws. Hey, that reminds me. How about, 'A stitch in time saves nine'? In other words, help me with this button."

For the first time, she noticed the threaded needle in his hand and the button hanging loose from his shirt.

"Hey, Dad. You're supposed to take the shirt off first."

"Not me. Why make it harder? Come on, Shel — help."

She grinned. For a sharp man, he was acting very helpless. And her mother, she realized, had quietly left the room.

"I should think an engineer would know the best way to put on a button," she challenged.

His eyes twinkled. "Oh, I get it. Everyone wants to see me make a fool of myself. Okay, you watch."

He eyed the button, the shirt, and the needle and then very neatly and efficiently sewed the button on himself. When he was finished he thumped his chest. "So?" he said.

"So, Dad — sew. S-e-w!" she spelled. "Mom hates mending and so do I. You must take after Linda, or rather, she must take after you. You two are elected from now on. You do it so well," she said sweetly, fluttering her eyelashes.

"Why, you little conniver," he said with mock horror. "You trapped me." He tested the button with his thumb and forefinger. "Good job though, I must admit."

They both laughed. Her father was really a good guy. She was so glad he was her father and that they were such good friends. He could be picky about things sometimes and he was often too opinionated, but those were minor faults, she thought. If she had to describe him in two words, she would choose witty and kind. Not a bad combination in any man, Shelly decided on her way up to bed.

What two words would describe me, she wondered, suddenly glum, thinking of the work ahead. Lazy and late? Sloppy and slow? Disorganized and dopey?

She put her head on the pillow and pulled the quilt up to her chin.

Tired and sad. The words popped into her head. Was she ever going to make it? Would life always be this hard? She tried to change her thoughts to something nice, something to fall asleep on. She tried to picture Nick's face and imagine the party Friday night, but Ryan's face appeared instead and she couldn't erase it. Memories came with it and all she could do was lie there helplessly remembering what it was like to be Ryan's girl. It took her a very long time to go to sleep.

Right after school she went up to her room equipped with a tall glass of milk, a big bowl of raisins, and six oatmeal cookies. She warned her mother ahead of time that she would need to be excused from evening chores.

"Okay, honey," her mother said. "But keep an ear out for the twins if they cry or anything tonight. Linda and I are going shopping at the mall. Tony said he was going out too. That leaves you and your father. He has a lot of extra work this week so he'll probably stay in his study all evening."

Shelly worked steadily until six, sorting the cards,

making an outline, trying to decide how she could stretch the material out. She would probably have to skim both books again for extra stuff to put in. It was going to be hard. She wished she had more books and articles to work with. As it was, she would have to make up another book title. That would be a real test of her imagination, she thought. Right after supper she would think of something. It's cheating! She tried to ignore the thought. After all, Miss Abbott had said six sources, so she had no choice.

All during supper she was quiet, trying to think of a book title that would sound real. How about *Saving The Whales*, she thought, or maybe *Whales In Trouble*? Did they sound too fake?

She asked permission to take her coffee to her room. Her mother usually hated food in their rooms; too often, she complained, she never saw the dishes again. Shelly knew she was the worst offender. Once cleaning under her bed she had found three bowls and two glasses, the glasses with some kind of icky gray mold in them. Tonight her mother had said yes, though, and Shelly carried the cup carefully up to her room.

She wrote title after title and then made up author's names and publishers. That was harder. She had to look in the bookcase to find out some real publisher's names. She finally decided on *Trouble At Sea* by James Southworth. When she realized it was quarter of nine, her heart sank.

What was she going to do? She felt like kicking herself all over the room. Why had she wasted so much precious time on a dumb title for a book that didn't even exist? Would she ever learn to organize her time? And how did you make a bibliography anyway? And did you put your footnotes at the bottom of the page or on a separate page at the very end? Miss Abbott had explained all that when she gave the assignment. Shelly was sure she had taken notes that day in class, but now she couldn't find them in her notebook.

She felt prickles of impatience and a trace of fear. This was really the pits. At the rate she was going, she would have to stay up all night.

Wait a minute. Rather than waste any more time trying to find those notes, she would ask Linda. Her sister could tell her easily; she was sure she had to do the same assignment in her junior year. Surely, she would be able to help. She jumped up from the desk and hurried across the hall.

"Linda?" she called. The door was open.

Then she remembered. Linda and her mother were at the mall. They probably wouldn't be back until eleven or so. Later, if they stopped for something to eat.

"Darn," Shelly muttered. "Now what am I going to do?"

She stood in Linda's doorway. She could see her sister's desk in the far corner near her drawing board. Somewhere, in one of her drawers, she could probably find something to help her. She was sure Linda had kept her best papers. If she had, they probably would be easy to find. Linda was so neat.

Everything *was* neat, extremely so. And she was in luck. Not only were there school papers in the bottom desk drawer but they were all in file folders, carefully labeled. And there was what she wanted: *English 9-12 (Compositions, etc.)*

It was a fairly thick folder. Somewhere within it, Shelly knew she could probably find a paper she could use as a sample. Surely Linda wouldn't mind once she explained. She closed the drawer and carried the folder to her own desk. No time to worry about what Linda would say now, she thought. I'll explain later.

She went through the papers one by one, checking headings, marveling at the small, neat handwriting and the ruler-straight margins. The papers had all been corrected but she noticed that Linda's mistakes had been very few. She had received nothing less than a B+.

Then she saw it: English — Mr. Hamilton
Room 201 — Research Paper
by Linda Barr

The title was: "Edna St. Vincent Millay — Poet and Genius."

Her first sentence read: "After reading 160 sonnets selected by the author in a book collection, I believe they represent some of the finest expressions of the human spirit and are unmatched anywhere in power, originality, and, yes, even genius. . . ."

Shelly sat still. One hundred and sixty sonnets? What were sonnets anyway? Were they books? Had Linda read that many books to do this one paper? She read further, finding the writing interesting, even if she didn't understand a lot of it. Sonnets, she discovered, were not books at all, but a kind of poetic form. She counted ten pages in all, full of quotes and tightly written information. Linda's writing was rounded and tiny. Her own handwriting was big and loose and scrawly. She often had to take care just to make sure it was readable.

Linda had left space at the bottom of each page and had listed her footnotes in order. The bibliography was the last page.

Shelly sat very still, her eyes glued to the paper before her. She tried to block the thought that was struggling to come to the surface, but her tired brain could not resist it.

Why not? She finally allowed the thought. Linda had Hamilton, not Abbott. It was all done — all ready. All I have to do is copy —

She felt her face grow hot and the prickles on her neck and arms returned.

I'll never finish "Whales" in time, she thought. I'll never get it right — I don't have enough time. All I have to do is —

Making up the book title was cheating too. Why not go a little further and be sure of a good mark?

She thought of what could happen. If she got caught, she could be kicked out of school, disgraced, and everyone would know. The thought was too horrible to consider.

That hateful voice whispered. Mr. Hamilton doesn't even teach at Enfield High anymore, so who's to know? I'll tell Miss Abbott I changed my mind halfway through and I didn't tell her because I was kind of embarrassed about being so interested in poetry. I'll tell her Grandma was a poet and she had all these books in my room and I just got hooked.

She stopped suddenly, shame and horror welling up in her. I'm using Grandma. I'm making up all these things and I'm really *using* her. She was amazed at how quickly and easily the lies had formed. She slapped the desk, suddenly angry.

Well, what else can I do? she thought. If I don't

do it, I'll fail for sure. She knew then what her decision would be. She just couldn't bear to pass in a hastily written paper, one that probably wouldn't even earn a C. She had to get an A. Linda didn't seem to have had any trouble. It just wasn't fair that Shelly should get less than her sister did.

So what if it wasn't her own work? She would make darn sure that Miss Abbott thought it was. She would even change some things, throw in a couple of misspelled words to make it seem more like her. She'd copy it over, of course, and by the time she finished writing, she would be an expert on this Edna St. Poet Person.

She cleared her desk, took some fresh white lined paper from her notebook, fished in her top desk drawer for her pen, and took two deep breaths. She began, taking care with her handwriting. She worked steadily, finishing pages quickly, all the while her tongue caught firmly between her teeth. At eleven-twenty she had reached the end. Her handwriting, larger than Linda's, had taken up sixteen pages. The finished product was satisfyingly thick and Shelly had even developed a sincere interest in the red-haired poet. The woman had really been ahead of her time.

She cleaned up her desk quickly, shoving the cards and papers from the abandoned whale project into her top left-hand drawer. Someday soon, she was going to have to clean that too, she thought. She replaced Linda's paper in the folder. She would return it right now and no one would ever know.

"You still up, Shelly?" It was Linda voice and her footsteps were coming up the third floor stairs. Shelly barely had time to shove the folder in her middle drawer before Linda appeared in the door-way.

"Wait until you see my new dress. It's fantastic! It was on sale, but who has to know that? It was marked down from fifty to twenty-five. Look at this label!"

Shelly looked at Linda. Was it possible that Linda liked the label more than the dress? Yes, she decided, it was possible. Linda worshipped quality.

What would she think if she knew what I was doing tonight? Shelly wondered. One thing for sure, she'd never understand. Linda would never let herself get into such a situation. Not her sister. She never would know what it was like to have her heart broken, hate her sister, and stoop to lying and cheating all in one week. Linda was perfect.

She forced herself to admire the new dress and make small talk for a few minutes. She wished with all her heart Linda would just get out of her room and leave her alone. She didn't want to talk or listen or think. She just wanted to fall into a deep, dreamless sleep and forget everything. Maybe tomorrow —

But tomorrow, she knew, wouldn't be any better. Everything was all mixed up, wrong. Nothing was as it used to be. She felt that she had become a totally different person almost overnight.

She put on the same flannel nightgown and decided against brushing her teeth tonight. It was just that she couldn't face herself in the bathroom mirror.

Once in bed, she found herself putting her thumb in her mouth, her forefinger automatically curling around her nose. She jerked her hand away, horrified. Thank heavens, no one had seen her. Why on earth had she done that anyway? I haven't sucked my thumb since I was three years old, she thought frantically. Why, even Angela doesn't do that. She lay stiff and straight, rigid with shame and sorrow. What's happening to me? she asked the dark room. What am I going to do?

Chapter 13

Linda took one look at her and groaned.

"You're not going to the party like that, are you?"

"Nick said informal," Shelly said, defending her outfit. A party, any party in Enfield, meant jeans or corduroys with a gauzy top or a good tee. It was almost a uniform. You couldn't go wrong wearing that.

"Listen," Linda said, her voice low and controlled. "*Your* casual is not Stinnett casual. I've been to a few parties there. College is different. The other girls, especially the ones from retailing, are going to be *dressed*. Don't you ever look at magazines, Shelly? *Mademoiselle*, or even *Seventeen*?"

"So what am I supposed to wear?" Shelly asked patiently.

"Not jeans! Come on up to my room. You have time before he gets here. Really, Shelly, you can't go like that."

Shelly followed meekly, wondering why Linda was acting like a fussy mother hen, not wanting her chick to make the wrong impression. Linda had never noticed what she wore on a date until last week. Now, suddenly, she was interested. Maybe Linda really does care about me, Shelly thought. Maybe she's afraid if I go to the party dressed all wrong I'll be embarrassed. Or maybe it's just because Nick is Howard's cousin and she doesn't want to be ashamed of me. She couldn't decide which was true.

She did decide to go along with whatever her sister said. Anyway, she couldn't get too enthused tonight about clothes — or anything else. She wished she could just stay home. It had been a horrible day. But she didn't want to think about that now. She wanted to forget the look on Miss Abbott's face when she handed in the paper. She remembered her own stomach doing flip-flops while she babbled on and on about "my grandmother's favorite poet." She had talked so much that she ran out of breath finally, almost like she had been running for miles. Telling all those lies had actually taken her breath away. It took a long time before her stomach settled down. Worst of all, she was sure Miss Abbott had seen right through her. That with her special powers she knew just what Shelly had done.

Later she told herself that it wasn't possible, that no one would ever know, and certainly not Miss Abbott. Her imagination was just working overtime. It was a case of nerves. She hated the heavy feeling of dread, though. What if she was caught? She tried not to think of it.

Worst of all, Shelly spotted Ryan in the cafeteria talking to Susan Spencer. He was way across the room, standing with Susan and two other girls, but he seemed to be paying strict attention to Susan.

Susan Spencer, of all people. Blonde and curvy. The girl who had been voted "prettiest" when they graduated from eighth grade. She was a cheerleader and vice-president of student council. In looks, Susan reminded her of Linda. Miss All-Around-Perfect.

She tried not to care. Besides, Ryan was only talking to her. He wasn't seriously interested in her, was he? Ryan had always told her *she* was his type. Still, she had worried all day. And the prospect of a date with Nick did not cheer her in the least.

Now, Linda had her looking "right" according to her own word. The tweedy skirt, the silky blouse, the sweater worn just so, the added blusher and pink eyeshadow all made her feel like an impostor. Nick would never get the chance to see her looking like Shelly.

"You don't look so Enfield High," Linda decided. "This town is about two years behind the real world."

Nick didn't do his mirror trick this time; in fact, he seemed to be in a big hurry. He barely looked at her as he helped her on with her coat. Conversation seemed even harder without Linda and Howard there. Shelly noticed how his smile kept turning into a frown, as if he couldn't make up his mind just how he felt.

Why, he's nervous, Shelly thought, and that knowledge made her less tense. All the way into Boston, she tried to make conversation, anything to have some sound. When she wasn't talking, the silence seemed too loud and embarrassing.

She asked questions about Stinnett, about his

subjects, the library, his professors. He answered unenthusiastically. He certainly doesn't sound too interested in the school part of Stinnett, Shelly thought. Instead, the only subject that seemed to turn him on was the party they were headed for.

"They let us hold these parties every month. We buy — uh — the liquid refreshment with our house fund. They don't say anything about it."

Shelly learned that Stinnett didn't have fraternities or sororities, only "houses." It mattered, though, which house you lived in. Nick actually didn't come out and say it but he hinted that his house was the best on campus.

Once they parked the car, Shelly had to walk fast to keep up with Nick. It was hard to do in her high-heeled shoes, and the wind whipping her legs was cold. She longed for her warm jeans.

"Slow down," she said. At this rate she would arrive alone.

"We're late," Nick muttered. "Party's already started."

So what? she wanted to say. What was the matter with him?

The minute she stepped into the huge foyer and took one look at the crowd milling around, she was glad Linda had talked her into changing her clothes. Even a quick glance told her no one had jeans on. Instead — and Linda was right — all the girls looked like they had stepped out of the pages of a current magazine. Perfectly-put-together girls, just like Linda. They all looked sophisticated, at ease. Shelly felt any anticipation drain out of her. She didn't belong here.

Their arrival hadn't caused any big stir. It didn't

seem like Nick was very popular. He took her coat and went off with it, leaving Shelly near the staircase. She felt awkward and shy. Was she supposed to just stand here like a lump? She noticed two girls eyeing her but their faces didn't look very friendly. Probably they're just looking me over to see if I'm anyone to worry about. She felt worse when they both looked away, disinterested. No one came over to her and she couldn't just walk over to one of those tight little groups and stand there like some kind of goop. Where was Nick? Why didn't he come back?

He appeared at her side, a can in each hand.

"I don't drink beer," she said. She didn't care what he thought. She had tasted it once and she hated it. It was sour and horrible, she thought. If she tried to force it, she knew she would be sick.

Nick looked disappointed. "Well, what *are* you drinking?" he asked, sarcasm in his voice.

"Coke or something," she said quietly.

He was gone again before Shelly could follow him. It was terrible standing alone. Couldn't he see how uncomfortable she was? She wandered around the hall, not daring to venture into either of the two, big, dimly-lit rooms for fear Nick would never find her.

She gazed at the framed photographs on the walls, hoping she looked calm and poised. The minutes passed and she began to feel really stupid. Darn Nick! How could he be so rude? Her dislike for him grew.

"Where do you go to school?" a voice at her side said.

Shelly turned. Standing beside her was an extremely small girl, her tiny eyes bright and birdlike. She wasn't a bit pretty but she was stylishly dressed. Shelly was immediately grateful for someone to talk to.

"I'm still in high school," Shelly admitted, but seeing the startled look on the other girl's face, she added, "I'm going to go to Stinnet, though."

The girl smiled. "Have you been accepted?"

Shelly hesitated. She would never see this girl again.

"Oh, yes," she said. "And I can't wait." Probably the girl was attending one of the many fashion or retailing schools in Boston. She had that look.

She was wrong. "I'm a junior here," Bird-eyes said.

"Oh," Shelly said, searching for something else to say. "Do you like it?" Maybe she could give her more information than Nick had.

"It's okay," the girl said.

Shelly had the awful feeling that the girl could see through her, that she had probed her brain and knew that Shelly was only a junior at Enfield High and had *not* been accepted at Stinnett.

Where was Nick? She couldn't believe his behavior.

"Excuse me," she told the girl. "I have to find my date."

She walked in the direction she thought he had taken and found herself in a dining room. A long table held plastic cups and soda cans, bowls of pretzels and chips. There were big, ice-filled tubs on the floor filled with beer. It shouldn't have taken him more than two minutes to get her a drink.

For the next hour she searched, going from room to hall and from hall to room. She felt lost, bewildered, angry. It was like a bad dream. No one spoke to her or even looked at her. It was as if she didn't exist at all. She made two trips to the bathroom just for something to do.

She spotted him suddenly, leaning in a corner, talking intently to a girl with a startling figure. The girl was gazing up at him and smiling. She saw Nick laugh suddenly and put one arm around her shoulders.

Shelly was mortified. Now what should she do? She just couldn't walk over and stand there. She would feel ridiculous, like an intruder. She turned her back and walked over to the refreshment table and poured herself a soda. She munched on a potato chip, trying to look casual. She tried to decide what to do next.

Suddenly, she was furious. Why did Nick even ask her to the party if he didn't plan to even talk to her? Ryan would never treat her, or anyone, like this. It was just plain bad manners, she thought. And Linda thought he was a perfect gentleman. Such a good catch!

She turned on her heel and walked quickly into the other room. She would find a place to sit and she would wait until Nick finished his flirting. When he did come, she would insist on going home right away. She hated this party. She felt out of place, neglected, unattractive. Apparently, Nick had found someone he liked better. Oh, she hated him.

She sat for what seemed like hours, each moment long and agonizingly boring, not looking at anyone, sure that everyone noticed her sitting alone, pitying her, making fun of the girl whose date thought so little of her.

By the time he appeared, full of apologies and

excuses, her insides felt like a dozen snakes were coiled and ready to strike.

"Take me home now!" she hissed, not caring if he hated her back.

He stood above her looking down at her. She wouldn't look at him.

"The party's just getting good," he hedged.

"I don't feel good," she said. "I really have to go home right away. I think I'm coming down with something." She bit the words off hard.

"Okay, okay. I'll get your coat."

She noticed he walked unsteadily. How many beers had he had? Oh great, she groaned inwardly, that's all I need.

She couldn't bear to talk to him in the car. She was cold and tired and close to tears. All she wanted was to get home quickly.

But not quite so quickly. Nick was driving too fast. He was hunched over the wheel, his head down. Who did he think he was? A racing car driver?

"Slow down, Nick, please," she begged. "I hate to go fast," she explained as pleasantly as she could.

"Fast? I'm not going fast," he said, not slowing down a bit.

The car seemed like a missile, hurtling through dark space. Streetlights, telephone poles, buildings all seemed blurred.

"Please, Nick, slow down. I mean it!" she said, now really ready to cry. She wished she had had the good sense to call her father long ago. Now here she was, trapped in a speeding car with an arrogant, spoiled stranger.

He grinned at her. "I'll slow down on one condition," he said.

"What?" she asked weakly.

"Slide over here beside me and keep me company."

"Will you go really slow then?" she begged.

"Sure. Don't worry about it." His words were slurred.

They drove the rest of the way in silence. She sat close to him and endured his arm around her shoulders. She didn't pull away when she felt his lips on her hair, even though she winced inside. What a phony he is, she thought. Ignoring me all night and now he wants to make out with me. He doesn't even like me and he must know I don't like him either. It didn't make sense. She hated having to sit so close, inhaling his awful aftershave lotion. It was blackmail, that's what it was. If it meant dating a jerk like Nick Kent, she would rather stay home the rest of her life. When he pulled up in front of her house, Shelly moved quickly to get away from him.

"Hold on a minute," he said, his face bending to hers. She caught a quick glimpse of his thin, hard lips and hurried to open the car door.

"I have to go right in," she said firmly. She pushed the door open and got out fast. She wasn't sure if he said anything more but she didn't wait to find out. She almost ran up the walk to the house. Just as she opened the front door, she heard his car pull away.

The warmth and friendliness of her own home comforted her. Safe and sound, she thought. As far as she was concerned, Nick Kent, from that wonderful family, could go pound salt. She never wanted to see him again.

Chapter 14

Sandy called her in the morning and Shelly gave her a detailed account of the evening with Nick. It helped to get her anger and disgust out in the open. She laid it on thick, making him sound totally evil, when she knew darn well now that he was just very immature and thoughtless. But it was fun making Sandy gasp and giggle. Before she was through talking, she was referring to Nick openly as "pickle-face," and Sandy was in stitches. It was mean of her to make fun of his looks, Shelly thought, but doing it made up for the humiliation she had suffered last night.

Shelly's good mood didn't last long. At lunchtime, Miss Abbott's name came up.

"I'm going to meet that teacher you like so much, Shel," her mother said.

"What? Who?" Shelly asked, startled.

"Your Miss Abbott. And your other teachers, too. It's Parents' Night Monday. Remember? I didn't get to go last time."

She panicked. Would Miss Abbott mention the research paper and the last-minute switch? If she said Edna St. Vincent Millay, Mom was bound to remember that Linda had done a paper on her. She couldn't let her mother go!

"Oh, Parents' Night is beat," she said. "None of the other parents go to it. I hear the lines are so long and you have to wait. You'll end up spending most of the time in the hall," she said.

Her mother looked puzzled. "If none of the other parents go, then how can the lines be so long? I don't understand you tonight." She looked at her. "Is there any reason why you don't want me to go?"

Shelly tried to look indifferent. "Of course not. I just thought I'd save you the trip. Everything's fine at school."

"Well, I'd really like to go. For you and Tony. I always like to meet my children's teachers," she said firmly.

Shelly felt hopeless. What was she going to do? She had convinced herself that there was no chance of being found out, no possible way anyone would know she had cheated, and now this.

She didn't hear what her mother said. "What?" she asked. The music on the kitchen radio suddenly seemed too loud and the twins' high voices grated on her nerves.

"I said, would you watch Angela and Eric this afternoon? Dad and I were invited over to the Hernons' for cocktails."

She stared at her mother's pretty face. Her expression was pleasant, mild, and Shelly knew that she expected Shelly to say "yes" as she always did. But why should she baby-sit all the time? They weren't *her* babies. She never had any time for herself. Everyone took advantage of her. No one cared what was going on with her or considered her problems. She didn't feel like playing with the twins today. She didn't want to be with *anyone.*

"What about Linda?" she said, aware of the whininess in her own voice. "She never has to do anything around here."

"Linda's going out with Howard. She said she'd be leaving around four," her mother said quietly.

"Yeah, and she'll need the time before that to get ready, right?" Shelly said.

She was aware of her mother's surprise, but she didn't care. Soon enough both of her parents would know what a truly horrible person she was, a cheat and a liar. They already knew how disloyal she had been to Ryan.

"Shelly, is something wrong, honey? Did anything happen last night to upset you? You're not yourself today."

"No," Shelly mumbled. She wished the twins would be quiet. They were babbling and Eric's windup toy screeched terribly.

"Do you two have to be so noisy all the time?" she said in a loud voice.

The babies looked up, their eyes wide and bewildered. She felt a jolt of shame. It wasn't *their* fault, she thought.

"Don't worry, Mom. I'll baby-sit. I always do, don't I?"

The words were out of her mouth before she could stop them. The minute she said them, she wished she could take them back. She hated the look of hurt that passed over her mother's face. She got up and went over behind her mother's chair and leaning over, wrapped both arms around her.

"I'm sorry, Mom, really. I guess I'm just tired and cranky. I did have a terrible time last night but I shouldn't take it out on you."

Louise Barr laid her cheek against Shelly's. "It's okay; I understand. We all have our bad days. But are you sure you're all right? It's so rare to see you in a bad mood."

If you only knew, Shelly thought. She hated to imagine the look on her mother's face when she discovered her daughter was a cheat. Would she be able to forgive her so easily then?

She left the kitchen and wandered aimlessly into the living room. The rug needed vacuuming and the fireplace was loaded with ash. It was almost two o'clock. Did her mother plan to clean in here before she left for the Hernons' or was she just assuming someone else would do it? That someone being Shelly? She felt the anger return. Who did everyone think she was? Cinderella?

Her father stopped on his way into the kitchen. "Hey, Shel. Whatcha doin'? Why don't you come and sit in my study for awhile. You and I haven't had one of our brilliant conversations for a long time."

"No thanks," Shelly said. "I have to clean up here. It's a mess."

His blue eyes darkened but he nodded once and went on to the kitchen.

Mom will probably tell him I'm in a rotten mood, she thought. They'll blame it on growing up—hormones or something. Anyway, she was relieved. It would be impossible to sit and talk with her father today. She wouldn't have been able to even meet his eyes. To her father, lying was the worst,

Shelly knew. And passing in your sister's work as your own was a very big lie. How could he understand that? She could imagine the hurt and disappointment in his eyes.

She grabbed the pile of last week's newspapers and began to roll them into logs for the fireplace. Her father had taught her how to do it when she was only five years old. If only she could be five again now, she thought. I didn't have a worry in the world then. If only she had the power to turn back the hands of time. If only she had never handed in that paper!

Two heavy tears spattered on the newsprint. She wiped them away angrily. It's too late to cry now, she thought.

Chapter 15

The rest of the weekend was a nightmare. By Sunday night she had given up trying to be part of the family; everything that was said or done seemed to be directed at her.

When Linda said she had to wash her hair — "I just did it yesterday and already it's so greasy" — Shelly was sure it was a slur against her. A hint that *her* hair was horribly dirty.

When her mother sighed and stretched and said she planned to go to bed early, Shelly knew it was because she hadn't helped her with dinner.

Even Tony and her father seemed to be extra quiet, a sign that she was depressing them with her long face.

She went to her room, closed the door, undressed, and crawled into bed. When morning came she turned over and burrowed deeper under the covers.

When her mother called up the stairs, she didn't have any trouble making her voice weak and hoarse. That's exactly how she felt. She wasn't lying when she told her mother she didn't feel good. She really didn't. Her head ached and her stomach felt crampy. It was a relief to huddle under the quilt all morning, half dozing, not really thinking. It was as if she were suspended somewhere in space. School and Miss Abbott were someplace far away. Parents' Night didn't exist. Only the big, warm bed had any reality. She wouldn't let her mother pull up the shades, and the room stayed dark and warm like some kind of safe cocoon.

She had tea and toast and some chicken noodle soup in the middle of the afternoon. Linda stopped in after school and brought her a new magazine to read, and the twins sent up their day's artwork to her. By six o'clock she felt better, but she continued to play sick. She had no desire to go downstairs and watch her mother get ready to go to Parents' Night.

Within a couple of hours she would know all about it. Her father, too. There wouldn't be any thrilling letter of acceptance from Stinnett next year — no look of approval and respect on their faces. Instead the Barr family would have to live down the disgrace of a dishonest daughter. Everyone would know.

She didn't want to think about it. She fiddled with the dial of the little white radio beside her bed. She wanted loud music now to drown out the thoughts that kept repeating and repeating in her head.

She was still in bed with the radio on and the lights out when she heard a sharp knock at her door.

"Come in," she called.

Linda opened the door and just stood there for a minute.

"Do you mind if I turn a light on?" she asked in a tight voice.

"Go ahead," Shelly said, puzzled, turning down the volume on the radio.

The sudden glare of the overhead light hurt her eyes and she blinked. Why was Linda standing so stiff?

Her sister's voice was cold. "Do you have my folder?" she asked.

Shelly froze. "What folder?"

"My school folder. The one with my English papers," she said.

"Why would I have it?" she asked, stalling for time. She could say she had borrowed it to find out about footnotes. That was true enough. Except very soon, her mother would be home and the truth would be out.

"It's missing," Linda said. "My things are out of order. That folder is gone. It was there just the other day. Now a whole stack of folders are upside down."

Shelly looked at her sister. Did she really check her desk drawers every few days?

"Do you have it, Shelly?" Linda asked again.

She threw back the covers and got out of bed, not looking at Linda. She opened the drawer and withdrew the folder.

"Here," she said. Linda was looking at her with a mixture of disbelief and scorn.

"You really took it? You went in my drawer and just took it?" Her voice was high and strained.

"I needed it for something," Shelly said flatly. She wished Linda would take her folder and get out of her room.

"Why would you want it, Shelly?" Linda said, curiosity in her voice.

Shelly shrugged. She *hated* this. "I said I needed it."

Linda's back was rigid. One hand was clenched tightly. "You know how I feel about my things. I'm entitled to some privacy. Would you like it if I went pawing through your drawers — and closet?"

Ah, she hasn't forgotten that, Shelly thought. "I didn't go *pawing*," she said defensively. "I needed some information right away and you weren't home." She paused. "I meant to put it back."

"What information?" Linda said and flipped through the papers in the folder.

Shelly looked at her sister. She looked incredibly neat and shiny clean in her blue-green robe and matching slippers. Her hair, as usual, looked freshly brushed and even without any makeup, her face was smoothly beautiful. Shelly felt her stomach tighten painfully. She knew she looked rumpled and seedy in contrast. It was unfair. Life was so unfair. All men, and all women, were *not* created equal, she thought. At least not Linda and I. We're sisters but she has it all. She'll always be way ahead of me and I'll always be sloppy, irresponsible Shelly — second best.

"Forget it," Shelly said wearily, rubbing her eyes. "It doesn't matter now. I did it and I'm sorry if you're mad."

"Listen, Shelly," Linda said. "This has been happening much too often. My room doesn't seem to be my room anymore. I'm going to have to talk to Mom and Dad about this."

Linda didn't really look angry, Shelly noticed.

In fact, her blue eyes were shiny, as if there were tears there, ready to fall. Her sister turned and hurried out the room.

Shelly shut the door and leaned against it, reaching out for the light switch. In the darkness Shelly suddenly felt real panic seize her.

Linda would tell about the stolen folder. Even if Miss Abbott didn't mention it, Shelly would have to explain why she needed Linda's work. Could she keep lying? Could she actually look her mother and father in the eye and tell the story about needing footnote information? She felt sick thinking about it. The panic was growing, spreading through her body. She couldn't stop pacing the floor. It was dark and she bumped into the big rocker and stubbed her toe hard. Pain shot through her and took away whatever control she had left.

She sat right down on the floor and put her face in her hands and cried, the tears splashing between her fingers. Over and over she repeated: Ryan, Ryan, Ryan. She needed him so much. She would give anything to put her head on his shoulder now and feel his strong arms around her. If he knew how she was suffering, he would care, wouldn't he?

"Oh, Ryan," she sobbed aloud. "I need you so much."

Without another word, she rose from the floor and turned on the bedside lamp. She found underwear, jeans, and a warm sweater and got dressed quickly. She found her boots in the back of the closet and put them on. She brushed her hair and grabbed her purse.

Her mother and father didn't like her roaming around at night. If she had somewhere to go in the evening, one of them would usually drive her, but tonight was different. She glanced at the clock. It was eighty-twenty. Buses ran past Carlton Road on the half hour. If she hurried, she could make it.

She went downstairs very quietly and took her heavy jacket and scarf from the closet. The door to her father's study was closed. She slipped out the front door and ran down the hill, not stopping until she reached the bus stop. She knew where she was going but she wouldn't allow herself to think about it. If she stopped to consider it too long, she knew she would turn around and run back home.

She was the only passenger on the bus until they reached Enfield Square. Then commuters from the train station crowded on, looking tired and haggard and in a hurry to get home.

Shelly was in a hurry too. She needed help so much. Her mind was sore and she thought if anyone spoke to her, she would start crying all over again and never be able to stop.

Kitty Gallagher opened the door and her attractive, freckled face clearly showed her surprise and concern. She reached for Shelly.

"For heaven's sake, child. Come in out of the cold. What are you doing here?" She poked her head out the door looking to see how her guest had gotten there.

"I came by bus," Shelly explained. "Is Ryan home?"

"Why, yes, he is." Kitty held her hand out. "Give me your coat."

Shelly hesitated. "Maybe I'd better keep it on. I may not be staying more than a minute."

"Let me have it," Kitty said firmly. "You're not

going anywhere until you thaw out. It's March but it feels more like December."

She took Shelly's hand. "Come in the kitchen. I always have tea on the back of the stove. Not that pale, bag kind but the real thing, strong enough to put hair on your chest." She laughed. "Not that you want hair on your chest." She handed Shelly a steaming cup.

Shelly tried to smile.

"Aw, I'm sorry. Making jokes when you've got something serious on your mind. Look, sit down, sip, and I'll get Ryan." She paused, her face grave. "Will he be glad to see you?"

"I don't think so, Mrs. Gallagher. But I hope he'll talk to me. I — " She felt tears spring to her eyes and she couldn't finish her sentence.

"I'll get him," Kitty said quietly.

She was beginning to feel some warmth in her fingers when Ryan appeared in the doorway. His blonde hair was rumpled and he was in his stocking feet. He looked at her steadily, not smiling.

"What is it, Shelly?" he asked. He reminded her of his mother at that moment.

She tried to meet his eyes but the calm steadiness of his gaze filled her with shame. She had hurt him so.

"Ryan?" she started. "I'm really sorry to bother you but I didn't know what — I mean, I didn't have anyone else to — " She felt her voice tremble and break.

He pulled out a chair and sat across from her. He spread both hands flat on the table and she remembered how many times he had sat just that way at her house.

"Go ahead," Ryan said. "I'm listening."

"I haven't any right. I mean, I know you probably don't want to hear my problems."

"Shelly," he said patiently. "What *is* the problem?"

She bowed her head. "I'm in big trouble at school. And at home, too. I've done something really awful. I didn't *plan* to. Everything just seemed to happen at once."

"Start at the beginning," he said. "I knew something was wrong that night at the movies."

He didn't sound mad at her. No matter what happened, she was glad she had come.

"It's hard to explain. It's hard to admit you're jealous of your own sister. So jealous I guess I wasn't seeing straight."

He nodded as if he already knew about it. "Go on," he said.

"Remember I even thought you liked Linda better than me? Remember how upset I was?"

He nodded again.

"Anyway, it goes back farther than that. It didn't just start, I mean. I've always felt that Linda was better than I was. Part of me hates her for it and the other half loves her. I want her to love me, too. I think that's why I said I'd go out with Nick last week. So *she* would like me. So we could be closer."

She saw his face tighten but he didn't say anything.

"I'm really sorry," she said softly, but his expression didn't change.

"Anyway, remember the paper about whales I was supposed to do for English?"

She told him as quickly and as simply as she could about what she had done.

"Don't you see? I thought if I could get a good mark then I would have a better chance of getting into Stinnett."

Ryan looked at her, his eyes glinting.

"You really want to be a doctor?" he asked.

She flushed. "Oh, I don't know. The truth is, I still don't know yet what I really want to do. I guess the doctor idea was just to show Linda and everyone else that I could be important too, that *I* was special."

"So you think Miss Abbott's going to blow the whistle on you tonight?" he asked.

She nodded sadly. "And Linda too, probably. Ryan, what should I do? I feel like just running far, far away."

He made a face. "That wouldn't prove anything. Or solve anything either. Listen, remember the time I dropped the tire iron on the Jaguar? Remember I told you what a big dent it made? I was scared. My boss has a bad temper. Anyway, I wasn't going to say I did it. You told me I'd better tell him about it. If he found out later, you said, he'd probably fire me on the spot." He smiled. "I'm giving you the same advice you gave me. Own up to it. The worst part of what you do wrong is the fear that someone will find out about it, right? I remember I walked around in a cold sweat until finally I just blurted it out. I waited for him to start yelling and cursing me out. Remember what he said to me?"

"Yes," Shelly said, encouraged by the friendliness in his voice. "He said, 'You're all right, kid.' "

"Well, he made me do extra work around the garage for the next week or two — all the dirty jobs, but he didn't fire me. That was the weekend

I was just too beat to take you out anywhere, remember?"

"So you think I should go home and tell them? Miss Abbott, too? Ryan, I could get suspended — even expelled. Oh, I can't." The thought of it made her shudder.

"Well, you can't walk around with this hanging over your head. It'll drive you crazy."

"I know. I'm so mixed up now."

"Listen, I'll drive you home. Your mom should be home by now and if she does know, then she'll be looking for you. You said your father didn't even know you left the house? They'll be worried. Hey, Shel. If it will help, I'll go in with you."

Suddenly she was in tears. "Oh, Ryan. You're being so good to me. I hated having you mad at me. I missed you so much."

He reached out and patted her hand. "I've missed you too, girl. I was hurt, I admit that, but now I know the whole story and I can't be mad anymore. I guess my pride was hurt the most. I thought maybe a mechanic wasn't good enough for you or something. I thought maybe you were getting like your sister."

"No," she said thoughtfully, truthfully. "I don't think the same way Linda does. We're different in that way."

"Good," Ryan said. "Now let's get you home."

She took her coat from Ryan, intending to put it on herself, but he held it open for her and when she backed up and put her arms in the sleeves, he suddenly had her in a fierce bear hug from behind.

"Oh, Ryan," she said. "I love you."

"I love you, too," he said softly. He led her out the door and into his old car.

She wouldn't let him come in with her when they got to her house. "I have to do this by myself," she said.

He smiled and kissed the tip of her nose.

"You're all right, Shel," he said.

Chapter 16

Her parents were sitting side by side on the couch in front of the fire. Their backs were toward her but something about the bend of her mother's neck and the slump of her father's shoulders told her that they knew.

The rest of the house was silent. Had Linda and Tony been told to stay in their rooms? She squared her shoulders and walked around to face them. She forced herself to meet their eyes, prepared to see anger and scorn. Instead, what she saw in Mom's eyes was relief.

"Where did you go? We were worried about you, Shelly." She sat forward and looked at Shelly searchingly. "You weren't wandering around out there in the dark, were you?"

"No. I took the bus over to Ryan's. He drove me home."

She realized her father's eyes had never left her face. He seemed to be waiting. Suddenly her legs felt weak. She sat down on the old leather hassock and put her hands on either side of her for support.

"I guess Linda told you about it, huh?" Shelly said.

"Linda?" Dad said questioningly. "We haven't talked to Linda. Did you tell her about it?"

Shelly was surprised. She had been sure Linda would go to her mother the minute she got home tonight.

"Well, not exactly," she murmured. She looked at her mother. "Miss Abbott, then?"

Her mother nodded sadly. "Your teacher was rather amused at first at your sudden change in topics, then after she read your paper she was very concerned. She said she knew immediately that it wasn't your work, your style. I remember Linda doing that report very well. I helped her find Grandma's books, in fact."

Her father cleared his throat. "Shelly, what made you do it? You had your own idea — a good idea, too. We talked about it and I remember you were very excited about it. You had all kinds of plans for researching it."

Shelly wished she could erase the hurt and puzzlement from her father's face with a few easy words. But the words weren't going to be easy. They would have to hear it all — how their own daughter was so terribly jealous that she would stop at nothing.

"Dad, Mom, it's so hard to explain. I mean, it didn't just happen on the spur of the moment. It has to do with the kind of person I am."

They waited.

"Well, you probably know all this but you don't say it because you're both too nice, but you have to know I'm not too good at anything. I'm disorganized, messy. I'm lazy and not talented at anything."

Her mother frowned and opened her mouth to speak.

"No, wait! Don't say anything yet," Shelly said. She had to say it all right now. She had to make them understand.

"I look at Linda and compare myself with her and I always come out second. She's prettier, she has a better figure, she's smart and talented. She's so neat, too. She's all the things I'm not. I know you see it, too. How could you not? It must be hard to have one daughter who is so perfect and then to have a second one who is — well — imperfect. It's wonderful that you never say 'Be more like Linda'; most parents would."

She paused, searching for the right words. "When we were little, I kind of felt sorry for Linda. She didn't seem to have as much fun as Tony and I did, but later — " She thought of something. "Mom? Do you remember that summer we went to Maine and you bought us new bathing suits? Linda's was a one-piece yellow and I wanted one exactly like it. You tried to persuade me to get a blue one with ruffles across the top but I wanted the yellow one. When we got to Maine and when we first went to the beach, I knew I had made a mistake. Linda looked great, the bathing suit was perfect on her. I ended up stuffing the top of mine with rolled-up socks. You and Dad pretended not to notice. He even called us 'The Gold Dust Twins,' but that was the moment I realized we were different, Linda and I. No matter how I tried in anything, I could never compare with her." She managed a smile. "I forgot about the socks that day. Tony chased me in the water and they got waterlogged and I had to throw them away. I wore the yellow bathing suit the rest of the summer, but every time I did — " She sighed heavily.

"Mom — Dad, I'm not trying to make excuses. All I know is that I was sick with jealousy. That's the truth. I wanted to do something to make you proud of me. I had to get a good mark on that paper because I had to get accepted at Stinnett next year and — "

Her father leaned forward. "Why Stinnett?"

"Well, if you had a daughter who was studying to be a doctor, wouldn't you be proud?"

He leaned back again and sighed. "You never mentioned wanting a career in medicine," he said.

She hung her head. "I know. But Linda thinks doctors are the *epitome*!

"So you were trying to impress your sister," her father said.

"And you, too. I figured if I can't be pretty and talented, maybe I can make my mark some other way."

"You're certainly capable of doing your own good work," her father said. "You didn't have to pass in Linda's work, did you?"

"Well, you see, that's another problem. I could have finished my project. I *was* interested. But I wasted time. I put it off too long. I just never — "

"That could be partly my fault, Shelly," her mother said. "I do ask you for help with the twins many times."

"That's not it," Shelly said. "If I have homework or other plans, I know I can tell you and you won't mind. A lot of times I know I have work to do, but I play with the twins anyway. It's my own choice."

"So you *chose* not to finish your paper on time," her father said.

"No, not really. At least I didn't think that I did that. The deadline was suddenly right there and I hadn't even started."

"So you took the easy way out?" he said slowly.

"Yes, Dad. But it hasn't been easy at all. I really *hate* what I did. I just proved what I always thought. I'm not as good as Linda. She wouldn't dream of doing what I did."

"No," her father said, "she wouldn't."

Shelly was stung. Her father was actually saying it — that Linda was better than she was. The words came out bitterly. "No. Precious Linda doesn't have to cheat or try to be something she's not. She's perfect and we all know it."

Her eyes were dry and the fear of crying had passed. Nothing she could say to her parents would help now. They knew what she was and they were stuck with it. She wished she hadn't listened to Ryan. Telling her mother and father how jealous she was, how mixed up, how stupid, was a mistake.

She had a sudden thought. If they told Linda that she was jealous, she would never be able to face her again. Pride welled up in her. *She didn't want Linda to know!*

She sat up straight.

"I just want to ask one favor of you," she said. "I don't want Linda to know what I said about envying her and all. It's none of her business."

Her mother moved, got up from the couch, and came to kneel in front of her. She put both hands on Shelly's knees. She looked directly into Shelly's face when she spoke.

"Honey, listen. First of all, neither your father or I consider you second best to anyone. It just isn't true. You are seeing things from your own particular angle but that doesn't mean that you are right. In fact, I'm telling you that you are dead wrong."

"How can I be wrong?" Shelly asked, her voice trembling.

"You don't see what we see. We have three daughters, okay? Every one of you is different. Three separate people. So different that it's really impossible to make comparisons, so we don't. But if we did, I would say that Linda has just as many problems as you do. Maybe more. Perhaps you can't see that, but I do. So does your father."

"You should talk to her sometime," Dad said.

Shelly was stunned. "What kind of problems could she have?"

Her father smiled, but there was more than a little sadness in it. "Maybe she wishes she were different. More like you, maybe."

"You're kidding," Shelly said. "Don't make fun of me."

Her father stood up and looked down at her. For the first time there was anger in his voice.

"I am *not* teasing you. Now do as I said. Go up now and talk, really talk to your sister. Make an effort. She's hard to get close to sometimes but that's what you have to try to do. If you want to get through to her, tell her exactly what you've told us tonight."

"Oh, Daddy, I can't," Shelly wailed. She pictured Linda's perfect eyebrows going up, a smug smile on her lips.

"Shelly, give her a chance," her mother said.

"Give Linda a chance? I'm the one who's going to get thrown out of school."

"About that," her mother said. "Miss Abbott did discuss that with me. She likes you and she said she would go to bat for you. You will definitely have to go to summer school though to make up English. She said since you've never done anything like this before, and because she thinks a lot of you, she is pretty sure the principal will listen to her." Her mother squeezed her hand.

"You'll have to work like the blazes next year if you want to get into Stinnett," Dad said.

Shelly looked at him. "I need more time to think about that," she said. "I'm not sure if it's something I really want. I mean, for me.

"Fine," he said. "You have plenty of time."

Her mother smiled at her. "We understand, Shel. We really do. We know what kind of person you are. Now just do this one thing for us — and for yourself. Go up and talk to Linda."

Shelly stood and touched her mother's arm.

"Okay," she said slowly. "I'll try. I don't think it will work, though. Linda will just laugh or something."

She started toward the stairway hesitantly and at the first step she stopped short, putting one hand on the wooden banister. It wasn't going to be easy to tell Linda that she was so jealous she couldn't see straight. In fact, it was the hardest thing she had ever had to do in her life!

Chapter 17

Linda was blowing on her fingernails when she opened her bedroom door. Shelly saw the polish, the remover, the file, and the orange stick arranged neatly on a paper towel. Everything just so, as usual.

Her sister held both hands out, the fingers spread. Her nails gleamed, a soft coral color.

"How do they look?" Linda asked.

"Perfect," Shelly said.

"That's what you think. I tried to pry the top off the powder can and I broke two of my best ones."

She held her right hand out. "Look closely," she urged.

Shelly didn't want to. A broken fingernail or two was not important now. She sighed and bent her head for a closer inspection.

"Oh, yeah. I see faint lines. Barely, though. How did you fix them?

"I have a special kit. You'd be surprised how often I have to use it. I do dumb things — like the powder can."

Shelly looked at her sister suspiciously. It was strange to hear her admit to mistakes.

"Did Mom and Dad talk to you tonight, Linda?" Shelly asked.

Linda looked up, a tiny frown between her eyebrows. "No. Why?" Shelly could tell she was telling the truth.

"I just thought . . ." She started timidly. It was going to be hard, standing like this, face to face.

"May I sit down?" Shelly asked politely.

Linda patted the side of her bed.

Shelly hesitated. "But you hate anyone to sit on your bed. You always said that."

Linda shrugged. "Only when the bedspread's on. It takes me so long to make it look just right, you know?"

Shelly sat uneasily. Linda tossed her a pillow and then she curled up daintily at the other end of the bed. The room smelled good, Linda's special scent rising all around her. She searched for a way to start the conversation. Nothing came to her so she decided to say it straight out.

"I used your Edna St. Vincent Millay paper, Linda. I copied it over and passed it in as my own. I meant to just use it for reference but mine wasn't even started and there was yours — all finished. So I went ahead and cheated. Miss Abbott told Mom about it tonight." She paused. "I was sure you had told her about the folder."

Linda's face was serious. "I was going to. I wanted to. It made me so mad thinking about it. I didn't dream you had copied anything, though. I was really worried about something else. I was afraid you — " Linda dropped her eyes, flustered, then looked up again. "I wrote some poems. Lots of them. I keep them in that drawer with the other folders. Did you read them?"

Shelly heard the fear in her sister's voice. "I swear I didn't. I found the Millay paper right off. I didn't see anything else. Honest."

Linda's delicate skin was flushed. "The poems aren't very good, really. But they're my way of getting things off my chest. Writing things down helps when there's no one to talk to." Her voice was very soft.

Shelly looked at her in surprise. "When do you ever want to talk to anyone? You're always in this room with the door closed. It's like you don't want anyone to bother you — like you don't want to be a part of this family."

Linda nodded and Shelly saw that her eyes were moist and shiny.

"I know," she said. "And that's how I often feel — not part of anything. I don't really fit anywhere, Shelly, not like you." She hesitated, not looking at Shelly. "I guess it's because I'm so darn shy. I'm afraid to say things out loud. You aren't. You say whatever comes into your mind and you don't even seem to have to think about it first."

Shelly snorted. "I put my foot in my mouth a lot. Sometimes I say some pretty silly things. I guess I don't think — "

Linda sat upright and her voice was excited.

"That's what I mean! You're not afraid to be natural. You roll around on the floor with Angela and Eric, getting all sweaty and dirty, and then Ryan walks in and looks at you and anyone can tell he thinks you're beautiful." She made a face.

"It takes me hours to look nice and when I finally do, Howard says, 'You look fantastic.' " But what would he say if he ever caught me with my hair dirty or without lipstick. Do you think he'd like me then? I don't think so."

"What you're asking is, would he like the real you?" Shelly said.

"That's the problem. I'm not sure who the real me is. I know I never can take it easy like you do. I can't relax ever. I worry all the time. I guess I feel like I have to prove myself." Linda's mouth trembled.

"But you have proved yourself," Shelly cried. "Linda, don't you know how much I envy you. You do *everything* right. You look perfect — you *are* perfect. You're so darn perfect, I can't stand it." She hesitated for a moment and then plunged on. "I guess I shouldn't say this, but sometimes I've really *hated* you."

Linda stared at her. "That's nothing," she said. "I've hated you, too.

Shelly stared back. "*You* hated *me*? Why on earth — ?"

"For lots of reasons. You don't worry. You know how to have fun. You have friends. You have Ryan. Mom depends on you. Dad loves to talk to you. You and Tony are really close and the twins adore you. And" — her voice was very soft — "you were Grandma's favorite."

Shelly's chest hurt. "Oh, Linda. She loved you, too."

"I know she did. She was always fair, but everyone knew that Grandma and Shelly were best pals. I used to listen to you two giggling in bed at night." Briefly, her eyes held a remembered pain. She continued: "Would you believe I take after Grandma in a lot of ways?"

Shelly thought about it. "Yes," she admitted, "you do." It all came back to her suddenly — Grandma's super-neat bureau drawers, her tidy desk and closet, her close attention to detail, and her meticulous personal habits.

"Maybe she loved you so much because you were just the opposite. Opposites do attract, you know," Linda said wistfully.

All at once Shelly saw her sister in a totally new way. Sitting cross-legged on the bed, her feet bare, she looked smaller, younger, more fragile — almost like Eric. For the first time, she noticed the bluish cast under Linda's eyes — the same thing that happened to her when she was sick or tired or when she had cried for a long time. She suddenly had an urge to touch her sister, something she hadn't done in years. If it was Eric, it would be so easy to just reach over and pat his face or gather him up in her arms and hug him, but could she — ?

Almost as if she were reading Shelly's mind, Linda leaped off the bed and danced away, her eyes sparkling with mischief. Now she looked just like Angela!

"You know what? Linda said. "Do you know what I've wanted to ask you for a long, long time?"

"What?" Shelly said, staring at Linda.

"I wanted to ask — I mean — would you like to go to Franklin's some night and get a big fat cheeseburger? And a double order of french fries and a chocolate shake?" Her blue eyes were hungry. "I've even been dreaming about it. Would you? Would you go there with me sometime?"

Shelly shook her head "yes" and laughed with

relief. "I thought you were going to ask me something horrible. Hey, you know me. I always like Franklin's. And they have Big Franks now. Double cheeseburgers with all kinds of stuff on them. They're *so* good!"

"Howard *hates* places like that," Linda said and giggled. "I thought I did, too."

Shelly stood up and stretched. "Maybe Dad would take us now. It's not really that late. He loves Big Franks, too."

"Oh, do you think he would?" Linda sounded like a little girl, Shelly thought.

"Let's ask him," she said, moving to the door. Then she stopped. She had to say it. "Linda, one thing I don't understand. You're usually so careful about your complexion."

"Yes, I am," she said seriously. "But I know you would just *love* it if I got big red pimples all over my face. You *would*, wouldn't you? Admit it!"

"Yes!" Shelly screamed, nearly choking on her laughter. That would be so *great*!"

They both laughed and then, together, they started down the stairs. Halfway down, still giggling, Shelly bumped into the banister.

"Ouch!" she said, rubbing her hip.

"Klutz!" Linda said affectionately.

"Okay, Miss Perfect! Shelly said.

They reached the second floor landing when Linda suddenly stopped. "I don't have my slippers on!" she said.

"Forget 'em," Shelly suggested gaily.

And Linda did.